"I'm never ge____ ____ ____" ____ said, jerking ____ ____ ____ ____ chest. "As of today, ____ ____ ____ letter word."

"Alan," Pamela said, leaning across the table, *"wife has always been a four-letter word."*

He frowned. "You know what I mean."

Pamela wondered what it would feel like to have a man so in love with you that he'd swear off marriage completely if he couldn't have you. It would be *so* romantic. Then she bit back a smile. Right now, with his hair mussed, his glasses askew and a narrow streak of mud on his jaw, Alan didn't exactly look the part of Romeo.

"What's so funny?" he asked, his expression hurt.

"Nothing," she said awkwardly, waving for the waiter to bring them more drinks. For the next half hour, while they drained their second pitcher of margaritas, they sat there extolling the virtues of being footloose and commitment-free.

At last Alan tossed a spent lime wedge onto the accumulated pile and looked at his watch, moving it back and forth as if he were trying to focus. "Time to go," he said, standing a little unsteadily. "I'm off on a honeymoon all by myself."

"Maybe you'll meet somebody," Pam suggested. *Why did that thought suddenly bother her?*

"Yeah, right." Alan started to walk away, then stopped as if he'd forgotten something. Then, turning back to her, wearing a sly, lopsided grin, he said, *"You could come with me...."*

Dear Reader,

Another Valentine's Day to celebrate with two very special LOVE & LAUGHTER titles. Popular Judy Griffith Gill has written another winning romantic comedy. Our hero is so convinced he has found the right woman for him when all she leaves behind is an ugly sandal that he begins the official Cinderella search.

Stephanie Bond continues her delightful duet with *WIFE Is a 4-Letter Word*. This time the groom who was abandoned at the altar in *KIDS Is a 4-Letter Word* finds his perfect match in the woman he least expected to love!

I hope Valentine's Day brings you both love and laughter.

Malle Vallik
Associate Senior Editor

Wife IS A 4-LETTER WORD

Stephanie Bond

♥ ♥ ♥ ♥ ♥

Harlequin Books

TORONTO • NEW YORK • LONDON
AMSTERDAM • PARIS • SYDNEY • HAMBURG
STOCKHOLM • ATHENS • TOKYO • MILAN
MADRID • WARSAW • BUDAPEST • AUCKLAND

ISBN 0-373-44037-5

WIFE IS A 4-LETTER WORD

Copyright © 1998 by Stephanie Hauck

Dear Reader,

Take one uptight computer geek who was just jilted at the altar, add one flamboyant blond bombshell who has a penchant for finding trouble, and you've got one calamity after another! If you read last month's *KIDS Is a 4-Letter Word,* you'll recognize Alan as the endearingly faithful boyfriend and Pam as the eccentric best friend. Only now they're sharing a week-long "honeymoon" in a nightmarish resort straight out of the seventies! Alan and Pam are the most unlikely pair imaginable, which only makes their romance more...*climactic.*

Thank you so much for supporting the LOVE & LAUGHTER line. I adore writing comedy, and I had a blast writing this story in particular. I hope *WIFE Is a 4-Letter Word* gives you many hours of enjoyment. (For you *Irresistible?* fans, you'll be glad to see a cameo appearance by a favorite character from that book!)

Drop me a note and let me know how I'm doing: Box 2395, Alpharetta, GA 30023.

Stephanie Bond

P.S. Don't forget to look for my first Temptation novel, *Manhunting in Mississippi,* available this spring!

This book is for Rita Herron,
who insisted that Pamela have her own story.

Many thanks to the Girl Scouts,
whose cookies arrived the week of my deadline.

1

ALAN PARISH DREW BACK and kicked the aluminum can high in the air, mindless of damage to his shiny formal shoe. Hands deep in his pockets, he watched the can bounce and tumble on the deserted rain-soaked sidewalk in front of him, gleefully imagining it to be John Sterling's head each time the metal collided with the pavement.

His mouth twisted with the ballooning urge to curse, but he couldn't think of an appropriate expletive to describe the basically nice guy who'd just happened to steal his fiancée—at the altar. Right now the only adjective for the man that came to mind was…smart.

Glancing around, Alan looked for something else to kick, suddenly wishing it were physically possible to make contact with his own backside. He should have asked Josephine to marry him months ago—no, years ago. Instead he'd taken their relationship for granted and she'd fallen in love with one of her clients, then canceled her marriage to him before his mother, perched on the front pew, had time to work up a good cry.

At this very moment, his friends and business associates were no doubt toasting the happy impromptu couple, at Alan's expense—literally. He winced, remembering that he'd made sure a case of his favorite champagne would be sitting behind the bar in the reception hall.

The sound of a speeding car approaching behind him, along with a telltale beeping horn, made him turn just as the vehicle zoomed through a curbside puddle and showered him from head to toe. Alan raised his arms in a helpless, deep shrug as the cold, muddy water seeped under his white shirt collar and dripped down his back. An aged white Volvo sedan jumped the curb a few feet in front of him and lurched to a lopsided halt, with one wheel up on the sidewalk.

Oh, well, he'd actually seen *worse* parking out of Pamela Kaminski.

"Sorry," she yelled, fighting and tugging her way out of the death trap she drove. "The hem of this damned lampshade dress got tangled in the pedals." She slammed the door and limped toward him. "Broke a heel, too," she reported.

Alan rubbed a finger over the lenses of his glasses to remove the water blurring his vision. Pamela should have looked ridiculous in the peach organza bridesmaid dress with the armful of stiff chiffon around her bare shoulders, but she didn't. With her typical irreverent air, and her remarkable good looks, she carried off the eighties prom-dress knockoff with panache.

From her alarmingly low-cut neckline, she dragged out a handful of white handkerchiefs. She then shoved back a strand of dark blond hair that had escaped her topknot, and began to swipe at the water streaming from his chin. "Sorry 'bout that," she murmured.

"No problem," he said tartly. "I needed to cool off."

She grimaced. "I was talking about the wedding."

"Oh." Trying to keep his eyes averted from the bosom of his ex-fiancée's best friend, Alan decided he'd never been more miserable in his life than at this moment. He stood completely still and allowed Pam to continue a woefully inadequate job of soaking up the water. "I can't believe Jo actually selected that dress for you to wear," he said sourly.

"She didn't," Pam said, painfully sticking the end of a hankie into his ear before moving on to swab his forehead none too gently. "Someone mixed up the order, but when it arrived, Jo seemed so stressed-out, I didn't want to bother her with it."

Alan scowled. "Since she only had eyes for John Sterling today, I'm sure she didn't even notice."

"It appears she did have a lot on her mind," Pam agreed.

Inhaling, then expelling his breath noisily, Alan said, "I suppose they got married."

Pam kept her eyes averted and nodded. "I heard Jo breaking the news to her mother just before I left."

"And you didn't stay?"

She pressed her full, brightly painted lips together and shook her head. "Between Jo, the groom and his three kids, I figured there were already enough people at the altar."

Grunting in frustration, Alan sputtered, "I can't believe after all these years of saying she didn't want children, Jo just up and marries a man with so much baggage!"

"Mmmnn," Pam said sympathetically. "*Three* carry-ons." She tossed the ruined handkerchiefs into a nearby trash can and pulled out her neckline, presumably to look for more.

Alan swallowed hard. He'd never thought about Pamela Kaminski romantically, but he was in the same pool as the rest of Savannah's male population when it came to admiring her generous physical gifts. The glimpse of a wildly inappropriate black strapless bra beneath the innocuous dress was enough to dry his tux from the inside out. When she plucked out two more hankies, he pulled a finger around his suddenly too-tight shirt collar. "Were you planning to shed a few tears, Pam?" he asked wryly.

She frowned and waved a hankie. "They were for Jo. The poor girl was crying like Niagara all morning."

"Thanks."

Pam glanced up and smiled sadly, her hands stilling. "I'm sorry, Alan. I didn't mean to hurt your feelings. I know how much you love Jo."

Anger, hurt and frustration welled up anew, so he cleared his throat and changed the subject. "Why did you follow me?"

She tossed the last two soiled handkerchiefs. "Thought you might need a friend. Where's your best man?"

"My guess is he's two choruses deep into the Electric Slide."

"Where were you headed?"

"To the airport."

She angled her head at him and laughed. "That's quite a walk."

"My flight to Fort Myers doesn't leave for four hours." He smiled tightly. "I allowed us plenty of time to celebrate at the reception."

"You're not serious," Pam said cautiously, as if she wasn't sure she was dealing with a sane person. "You're still going on your honeymoon?"

"Sure." He shrugged, then lifted his chin. "Why not? It's paid for. I'll drown my sorrows in buckets of margaritas on the beach. I plan to eat enough limes to stave off scurvy for a lifetime."

Pam stared at him, the blue of her eyes startling against the wide whites. Then she blinked and looked up as a large raindrop dripped down her cheek. Within a few seconds, the rain was pelting down.

Which Alan didn't mind since his day couldn't possibly get any worse.

Suddenly a bolt of lightning streaked through the sky and

struck a stand of trees several hundred yards away. On the other hand, perhaps he shouldn't tempt fate.

Pam was already tugging him toward her car. "I'll give you a ride. Where's your luggage?"

"In the back of the limousine at the church. I'll buy everything I need when I get to Fort Myers." He opened the passenger-side door, lifting it out and up at its awkward angle, then gingerly lowered himself onto the dingy sheepskin-covered seat. Once inside, he turned to look at Pam, who barked, "Buckle up," as she started the engine.

With a teeth-jarring jolt, they descended from the curb in reverse. Then Pam peeled rubber on the wet pavement, and made an illegal U-turn. As they sped toward the highway, Alan winced at the sound of her stripping gears, then braced an arm against the cracked vinyl dashboard. A dislocated shoulder was the most minor injury he could hope for when the rescue team extracted them with the jaws of life.

"Uh, Pam."

She glanced over at him, turning the steering wheel in the same direction. He gasped as the car ran off the shoulder, then sighed in relief when she jerked it back to the pavement. "What?" she asked, oblivious to his alarm.

"Never mind," he said hurriedly. "We'll talk when we get to the terminal. Do you know where you're going?"

She scoffed and made a heart-stopping weave across the yellow line, then yanked the hem of her dress above her knees. She was barefoot. "Alan, you know I practically live in my car. It's my *job* to know where I'm going."

Alan now realized why Pamela was the most successful real estate agent in Savannah—after a ride with her, prospective home buyers were probably too rattled to refuse.

To his horror, she reached over to tune the radio, and after enduring a full fifteen seconds of her not once looking at the road, Alan lurched forward and offered to find a station. He tuned in to some light rock and eased back in his seat, trying to relax.

Pam made a disapproving sound. "Is that all you can find? My *dentist* plays that stuff, as if the sound of a drill isn't torturous enough."

Alan sighed and found a more trendy station, assuming Pam was satisfied since she began singing along—badly. Suddenly he focused on the windshield wiper on his side and pursed his lips. "Is that a man's sock?" he asked.

"Yeah," she sang, weaving and shrugging. "The wiper blade fell off and the sound of that metal arm scraping against the windshield wore on my nerves."

Alan shivered.

She turned a dazzling smile his way. "The black sock is hardly noticeable and it works great."

He begged to differ, but he didn't dare. He briefly wondered which of Pam's admirers had left the handy souvenir, then pushed the thought aside. Instead, he closed his eyes and conjured up visions of sandy beaches and unlimited quantities of alcohol. He'd buy and finish the entire set of a new science-fiction series he'd been yearning to read. And Mrs. Josephine Montgomery Sterling, mother of three, would be far, far away...wiping runny noses.

Pamela respected his silence, humming and singing along with the radio, but not pressing him into conversation. After several minutes, he opened his eyes and glanced at her. Her profile was almost classically beautiful—the tilt of her nose, the curve of her pronounced cheekbones. Except Pam's upper lip protruded slightly over her lower lip, giving her the appearance of having an upside-down mouth. Combined with large blue eyes and a mane of dark gold hair, she was stunning to the point of being intimidating.

She had the braver half of Savannah's bachelors running to her bed, and the smarter half just plain running.

He'd heard the stories in the locker room at the club—Pam's exploits in bed were legendary. But he'd often wondered how many of the rumors were rooted in fact and how many were pure conjecture based on Pamela's background. She'd grown up in the Grasswood projects, the black eye of Savannah's otherwise beautiful downtown face. Grasswood was notoriously populated with several generations of dopeheads, prostitutes and petty thieves.

The first time he met Pamela, he'd peeled her off another girl's back in the hallway of his private high school and she'd rewarded him with a sharp kick to his shin. In response to public pressure, Saint London's Academy had extended scholarships to a handful of families from the projects, and Pamela's was one of the lucky ones. He remembered her two brothers being hoodlums and she herself being garish and unkempt, mouthy and irreverent, courting fights with girls, boys and teachers alike. One by one, the Kaminskis had all been expelled.

When he'd started dating Jo several years later, he'd been amazed to learn the girls were best friends, and more stunned still when he discovered that dirty-faced, sparring Pamela had become a top-producing agent for Savannah's largest realty company. Jo took Pam's flamboyance and reputation in stride, and soon Alan had grown more relaxed with Pam's company, despite her unpredictable and scandalous behavior.

The first time Jo had asked him to accompany Pam to a charity benefit as a favor, he'd been slightly uncomfortable, hoping desperately his high-bred mother didn't get wind of it because he didn't want to listen to her reproof. But he'd watched with fascination as Pamela the sexy siren had morphed into a sleek and charming conversationalist as she worked a roomful of potential clients. As a bonus, she'd even procured him a few introductions that had proved beneficial in advancing his computer-consulting business.

She was as different from his reserved, proper ex-fiancée as night and day. Jo was a quiet reading bench, Pam was a tousled bed. Jo was a contented house cat, Pam was a prowling lioness.

Alan frowned. The woman *was* a little scary.

"I'll wait with you," she announced as she veered into long-term parking.

"That's not necessary," he said, hanging on while she took him on a harrowing ride through the parking garage.

They lurched to a crooked halt one-eighth of an inch from a four-foot round concrete pillar. "I'll buy you a drink," she said, and lifted herself out of her seat with the force of putting on the emergency brake. "Let me get some decent shoes."

Hiking up her skirt, she walked around to the trunk in stocking feet. Alan got out of the car and followed her. She unlocked and lifted the lid to reveal an unbelievable array of footwear—pumps, sandals, boots, tennis shoes—he guessed there were fifty or more pairs scattered to the far corners of the trunk, no doubt from her perpetual careening.

"Do you moonlight as a traveling shoe salesman?" he asked.

She laughed. "I never know what kind of terrain I'll be showing a house in—I try to be prepared."

Alan reached in and withdrew a thigh-high red-patent leather boot. He lifted an eyebrow and asked, "Where's the matching leash?"

She smirked and yanked the boot away from him. Pam hastily rummaged through the pile and came up with one light-colored high-heel pump and slid her foot into it, then stood on one leg while she searched for its long-lost mate.

"Aha!" she said, finally retrieving it, then tossed in the pair with the broken heel and slammed the trunk with vigor. It bounced back up and she slammed it twice more before it held. "The catch is tricky," she informed him, slinging her purse over her shoulder. "Let's go."

They garnered more than a little attention as they made their way through the airport and settled into a booth at a tacky lounge. To send him off right, Pam ordered a pitcher of margaritas on the rocks, then poured one for each of them. She licked the back of her hand and sprinkled salt on it. He did the same and lifted his glass to hers.

"You make the toast," she said, her eyes bright.

Her beauty struck him at that moment, and his tongue stumbled slightly. "Uh, to being single," he said, clinking her glass heartily.

"I'll drink to that," she seconded, then downed half her drink, licked the salt from her hand and sucked on a lime wedge.

He followed her lead, squinting when the sour juice drenched his tongue. "I really didn't want to get married anyway," he mumbled.

"So why did you propose?" she asked.

Alan shrugged. "It sounds silly now, but at the time it seemed like the thing to do."

Her look was dubious, but she didn't question him further. Instead, she laughed. "You're a mess."

Alan glanced down at his wet, disheveled tuxedo and chuckled, then scanned her rumpled appearance and grinned. "So are you."

They both laughed and he loosened his bow tie, letting the ends hang down the front of his stained, pleated shirt. "What a hell of a day," he said, shaking his head and cradling the frosty glass of pale green liquid.

"Yeah," she agreed. She swallowed the rest of her drink,

licked her hand and sucked a fresh lime wedge. "Did you have any idea she was hung up on John Sterling?"

He frowned. "I knew he was hung up on *her,* but I never suspected she'd even consider a man with so many kids." He finished his drink, licked, then sucked. "Did you know?"

She shook her head and refilled their glasses. "I knew something was bothering her, but I assumed it was just prewedding jitters." She lifted the glass and downed a good portion of the margarita. He watched with interest as her tongue removed more salt from her hand. She sunk small white teeth into the lime and her cheekbones appeared as she drew in the juice.

"I feel like a fool," he announced, swallowing more of the tangy drink and performing the same ritual. "I know everyone is laughing at me."

She shook her head again, dislodging another strand from her stiff hairdo. "They probably feel sorry for you."

"Oh, thanks, that makes me feel *tons* better."

"Everyone will forget about it by the time you return," she said in a soothing tone as she topped off their glasses again.

The alcohol was beginning to take effect on his empty, nervous stomach. His tongue and the tips of his fingers were growing increasingly numb. He pushed his water-spotted glasses back up on his nose. "I hope so, but I doubt it. Maybe I should move."

She scowled, an expression which did not diminish the prettiness of flushed cheeks and flashing eyes. "That's ridiculous—you've lived in Savannah all your life. Your parents would be hurt. And your consulting business—" she lifted her glass again and squinted at him "—you can't leave before you get old Mr. Gordon's computer account.

I went to a lot of trouble linking up the two of you at the children's benefit.''

"I know," he said mournfully, swirling the liquid in his glass before taking another deep drink. "You're right, of course. But let me wallow a little—my ego is pretty tender at the moment."

"You'll bounce back," she said with confidence. "There'll be debutantes lined up at your door by the time you return from your trip."

Her words were slightly slurred—or was his hearing becoming somewhat warped? "Nope." He sat up straight and jerked his thumb to his chest awkwardly. "I'm never getting married. As of today, *wife* is a four-letter word."

"Alan," Pamela said, leaning forward, "*wife* has always been a four-letter word."

He frowned. "You know what I mean."

Feeling a little tipsy herself, Pamela looked across the sticky table at her drinking companion and a feeling akin to envy crept over her. She wondered what it would feel like to have a man so in love with you that he'd swear off marriage completely if he couldn't have you. Pam bit her bottom lip. She'd known Jo Montgomery for years, and her best friend had always demonstrated remarkable good sense—until today.

What could have possessed her to abandon her faithful boyfriend of three years at the altar to marry a widower with three kids? Granted, Jo had confided that her and Alan's sexual relationship left a little to be desired—and personally, Pam found Alan quite bookish and dull, but even a boring man didn't deserve to be jilted. But she knew Jo felt bad because she'd asked Pam to go after him. Even though she didn't say it, Pam knew Jo feared Alan might do something impulsive and self-destructive.

She watched as Alan tilted his head back and emptied

his glass. In high school, Pam had triumphantly dubbed him "the Ken doll", a nickname she still used in conversations with Jo, much to Jo's consternation. His fair hair was cut in a trendy, precision style, and his round wire glasses were like everything else in his wardrobe: designer quality.

The man was painfully clean-cut, his skin typically scrubbed within an inch of its life, his preppie clothes stiff enough to stand in a corner. She perused his slim, chiseled nose and squared-off chin, complete with an aristocratic cleft. He was handsome in an Osmond kind of way, she supposed, but everything about him screamed predictable.

Alan Parish came from thick money, as her mother would say. She doubted if he'd ever experienced belly-hurting hunger, missed school because his shoes had finally fallen completely apart, or scraped together money to post bail for three family members in one week. The worlds they came from were so far apart, they were in separate dimensions.

Then she bit back a smile. Right now, with his hair mussed, his glasses askew and a narrow streak of mud on his jaw, he looked more like one of her stray lovers—disorderly and disobedient. Only she knew better. Alan was an uptight computer geek—she'd bet the man had a flowchart on the headboard of his bed.

"What's so funny?" he asked, his expression hurt.

"Nothing," she said as fast as her thick tongue would allow while waving for the waiter to bring them more drinks. Then they spent the next half hour extolling the virtues of being footloose and commitment-free while they drained the second pitcher.

At last, Alan tossed a spent lime wedge onto the accumulated pile and looked at his watch, moving it up and back as if he was trying to focus. "Time to go," he said, standing a little unsteadily.

Pam stuck out her hand. "I think I'll stick around and sober up for the drive home."

"With your driving, who could tell?"

She scowled. "Have a great time, Alan."

"Yeah," he said dryly. "I'm off on my honeymoon all by myself." He bowed dramatically.

"Maybe you'll meet someone," she said.

Alan straightened, then frowned and pursed his lips.

"What?" she asked, intrigued by the expression on his face.

"Go with me," he said.

Pam nearly choked on her last swallow of margarita. *"What?"*

"Go with me," he repeated, giving her a lopsided smile.

"You're drunk," she accused.

He hiccuped. "Am not."

"Alan, I'm *not* going on your honeymoon with you."

"Why not?" he pressed. "My secretary booked a suite at a first-rate hotel, and it's all paid for—room, meals, everything." He pulled the plane tickets from inside his jacket and shook them for emphasis. "Come on, I could use the company and you could probably use a vacation."

A week away from Savannah was tempting, she mused.

His smile was cajoling. "Long days on the beach, drinking margaritas, steak and lobster in the evening." He wagged his eyebrows. "Skimpily dressed men."

At last he had her attention. "Yeah?"

He nodded drunkenly. "Yeah, you might get lucky."

But she couldn't fathom spending a week with Alan, and she'd *never* share a bed with the man, no matter how roomy. She shook her head. "I can't."

"I'll sleep on the pullout bed," he assured her.

She set down her drink. "But what will people think? What will *Jo* think?"

"What do you mean?" he asked.

Pam squirmed on the uncomfortable bench seat. "Well, you know—us being together for a week."

His shocked expression didn't do much for her ego. "You mean that someone might think that we're...that we're...*involved?*" His howl of laughter made her feel like a fool.

Of course no one would jump to that conclusion—a high-bred southern gentleman and a trashy white girl from the projects—it was ludicrous.

"And as far as Jo is concerned," Alan continued, "if she ever thought there was a remote possibility we'd be attracted to each other, she'd never have trusted me to escort you to your business functions."

Pam's fuzzy brain told her an insult was imbedded in his rambling. "I suppose you're right, but a few people might jump to conclusions."

Alan shrugged. "It's not like the whole town of Savannah is going to know, Pam."

She glanced down at the horrid peach-colored dress. "But I don't have any clothes."

"We'll go shopping when we get there," he said simply. "Come on, will you go or won't you?"

She had accrued vacation time. And only one deal in progress that she could probably handle over the phone. And Jo *had* asked her to keep an eye on Alan. She pressed a finger to her aching temple. It hurt to think too deeply.

Pamela emptied her glass and wiped the back of her hand across her mouth, then looked up at him and smiled. "Well, I could use some new sandals...why the heck not?"

2

ALAN SALUTED the head flight attendant, then dropped into his seat, wincing when the jolt threatened to scramble his furry brain. He felt as if he was forgetting something, but the answer hovered on the fringe of his memory, eluding him. His neck suddenly felt rubbery. Laying his head back, he closed his eyes and slowly reached up to pat the wallet in his breast pocket. That wasn't it. Hmm, what then?

"Ex-schuse me," came a loud female voice. He opened his eyes a millimeter and Pamela Kaminski slowly came into focus, just as her purse whacked some poor business-man upside the head. "Sorry, sweetie." She leaned over to place an apologetic kiss on the man's receding hairline.

Alan smiled and tried to snap his fingers, but missed. Pamela! He'd forgotten Pamela.

"There you are!" Pamela said, her eyes glassy. "When I came out of the ladies' room, you'd disappeared. Thank God, my middle name is Jo. Then all I had to do was convince a woman at the gate that the last name on my license and the name on the ticket were different because I'd just gotten married." She giggled. "Whew!" She swung into the seat next to Alan, then leaned against him and squealed. "I've never flown first-class before."

"Unlimited drinks," he informed her, rolling his head.

Her grin was lopsided. "No fooling? I'm up for another pitcher."

"You'll have to settle for one drink at a time—and they don't serve margaritas."

She pouted, sighing at the inconvenience, then noisily fumbled with her seat belt until Alan lifted his head and offered to help. "It's twisted," he announced, reaching across her lap to straighten the strap. The chiffon ruffles at her plunging neckline tickled his jaw. He valiantly tried to concentrate on the silver buckle, but his eyes kept straying to her cleavage. The tiny embroidered rose front and center on her black bra made an appearance every time she inhaled. After three clumsy attempts, he finally clicked the belt together, then settled back into his seat heavily.

The flight attendant eyed them warily when they ordered bourbon and water, but served them promptly enough. They finished the weak drinks before takeoff, and Alan found himself beginning to doze as they taxied down the runway. An iron grip on his arm startled him fully awake.

Pamela's left hand encircled his right wrist so tightly her knuckles were white. Her long peach-colored nails were biting into his flesh. And her face was turning as green as the many limes they'd sucked dry.

"What's wrong?"

"Remember when I said I'd never flown first-class?"

"Yeah."

"Well, I've never flown before, period."

"No kidding? Why not?"

"I just remembered—it's a phobia of mine." She put her fingers to her mouth. "Oh, dear."

He leaned forward and twisted in his seat. "What?"

"I'm going to throw up."

Alan panicked. "Oh, don't do that."

Still holding her mouth, she nodded in warning, her eyes wide. Alan fumbled for the airsick bag, and jerked it under her mouth just as the plane banked. She unloaded, missing the bag more than hitting it, although Alan accepted some of the blame for holding the paper bag somewhat less than stone still. He heard a groan go up from surrounding passengers.

When her retching gave way to dry heaves, Pamela slumped back into her seat, frightfully pale. A flight attendant was at their side as soon as the plane leveled off, extending a warm, wet towel to Pamela. "I'm going to need more than one," Pam muttered, eyeing the mess she'd made.

Organza was more absorbent than it looked, Alan decided, fighting the urge to vomit, himself, as he handed the bag to the attendant. Insisting she was too weak to make a trip to the lavatory, Pam cleaned up as well as she could sitting in her seat. The attendant, obviously at a loss, murmured the two-hour trip would pass by quickly.

"Oh, God," Pam breathed, laying her head back. "It's an omen—I should have never gotten on this plane."

"Relax," Alan said, reaching forward to pat her arm, then decided it would be more sanitary to pat her head. Her hair was stiff and had pulled free from the clasp that hung benignly above one ear. "It'll be a smooth flight—I travel all the time and I've never had any problems."

Suddenly the plane dipped, then corrected, then dipped and banked again. The Fasten Seat Belt sign dinged on, and the pilot's voice came over the intercom. "Ladies and gentlemen, we have encountered some turbulence." The attendant was thrown out of her fold-down wall seat, but she recovered and continued smiling as she fastened her own belt. "Please bear with us while the captain climbs to a higher altitude."

It was the worst flight Alan had ever experienced. The plane continued to pitch and roll, eliciting gasps and moans from the passengers. A cabinet door in the small galley gave way, sending trays of food into the aisles.

Alan felt terrible, willing his stomach to stay calm, and pressing his throbbing head back into the seat to keep it as immobile as possible. He felt terrible, too, for inviting Pam to come along. She'd probably be traumatized for life. He heard others seated around them getting sick, and he glanced anxiously at Pam to see if she would lose it again.

Her eyes were squeezed shut, and her lips were moving. "Hail Mary, full of...full of gr-grace..." She opened one eye and whispered to Alan, "I've never said my prayers while I was loaded—do you think it cancels out?"

Alan pursed his lips and considered the question, then shook his head and she continued to stumble through the prayer, finishing with "Pray for us s-sinners now and...and at the hour of our death. Amen." Then she crossed herself.

"Hey," he whispered soothingly. "We're going to be fine. It'll level out here in a few minutes."

On cue, the plane made a sickening dip. Pam swallowed and jerked her head toward him. "Are you crazy, Alan? We're all going to die and I'm going to be buried in this horrid dress—*if* they find our bodies."

He sighed. "Of course they'll find our bod—" He stopped and shook his head to clear it. "Wait a minute— we're not going to die, okay? I refuse to die in a plane crash on my wedding day."

Her eyes widened and she gestured wildly with her hands. "Oh, Mr. Moneybags, I suppose you're going to buy your way out of this?"

Alan frowned. He'd spent his entire life trying to make his own way, only to be frequently reminded he was a Parish, and therefore was forced to share the credit for his accomplishments with his family name. He crossed his arms, closed his eyes and refused to be provoked. "I'm not

going to argue with you because I'm drunk and tomorrow
this conversation won't matter.''

"Does anything affect you, Alan?" Pam asked, her voice
escalating. "You got jilted today and you still came on this
honeymoon like nothing happened. Now we're getting
ready to crash and you sit there like a dump on a log.''

"That's lump," he corrected, his eyes still closed. "A
lump on a log. Or is it bump?''

"I meant what I said," she retorted. "I'm drunk, but I'm
not incoherent...I'm...I'm...oh, God, I'm going to be sick
again.''

His eyes snapped open. He reached for the airsick bag
on his side and thrust it under her chin. "Arrgghhh!" he
cried when she missed the bag again. He looked away and
tried to reach the attendant bell with his elbow. Once the
remaining contents of her stomach appeared to have been
transferred to the bag, the floor and all surfaces in between,
she fell back into her seat, completely exhausted. At last
the pilot located a more comfortable altitude, and the turbulence ceased. The passengers cheered, and within seconds, Pam fell into a deep sleep.

Alan surveyed his traveling companion and winced. If
his head didn't hurt so much, he'd probably be laughing.
Pam Kaminski, the perpetual playmate, looked like a rag
doll in her stained, smelly, ugly gown. Her hair was lank
and damp, her mouth slack in slumber. He flagged the busy
attendant and quietly asked for more towels, then carefully
leaned toward Pam, trying not to wake her.

With fierce concentration, he delicately wiped her face,
admiring the fine texture and translucence of her creamy
complexion, and the long fringe of lashes on her sleep-
flushed cheeks. She never once stirred, not even when he
dabbed at the corners of her upside-down mouth. But for

the first time ever in the presence of Pamela Kaminski, Alan felt *himself* stir.

He shifted in his seat, trying to stem the rush of inappropriate feelings for his ex-fiancée's best friend. But sitting there in her mussed gown with her mussed hair, she looked like the grubby little tigress she'd been in high school, all piss and vinegar, and she made his blood simmer.

Passing a hand over his face, Alan blamed the lapse on his own lingering drunkenness. He hadn't made a big enough fool out of himself already today—why not make a pass at Pam and watch her laugh until she vomited again.

PAM WAS A BIRD flying over a landfill, dipping and diving, the stink of rotting trash permeating the air. She started awake and blinked, disoriented at first, then realized with a jolt that she was on a plane hurtling toward a shared honeymoon with Alan Parish, and that the stink was *her*.

"Ugh." She wrinkled her nose in disgust, and pulled herself straighter in the seat, flinching at the explosion of pain in her temples. She turned her head oh-so-slowly to see Alan zonked out, snoring softly and leaning against the wall. His expensive black tux was probably beyond cleaning, but his mottled jacket still lay folded neatly across his lap. Embarrassment flooded her when she remembered how he'd held the airsick bags as she filled them. She smiled wryly. Alan had surprised her.

A ball of white fuzz dangled in his hair, and she reached forward impulsively to remove it. Awareness leaped through her when she touched the silky blond strands, which was almost as alarming as the feeling of warmth that flooded her as she watched his chest rise and fall. Awake, he was Alan the Automaton. But relaxed in sleep, he looked downright sexy. A memory surfaced…she'd had an absurd crush on him for the short time she had attended the private school his family practically owned.

Before she had time to explore the amazing revelations, the attendant who had earlier emptied the linen closet on Pam's behalf, touched her arm and murmured, "Are you feeling better, ma'am?"

Pam nodded gingerly.

The woman smiled gently. "I'm sorry, Mrs. Parish—this flight wasn't a very promising start to a honeymoon."

Confusion clouded her brain. "But I'm not—" She glanced up at the woman and smiled tightly. The situation was too convoluted to explain. "It'll be fine once we get to Fort Myers."

"Congratulations—was it a long engagement?" the woman pressed.

"N-no," Pam stammered, suddenly nervous. "This was all quite sudden. Could you direct me to the bathroom, please?"

The blue-suited attendant pointed and smiled, then walked back down the aisle.

Pam slowly pulled herself to a standing position, but the movement stirred up a fetid smell from her dress. Swallowing her urge to gag, she gathered her skirt in her hands, hiked her dress up to her knees and sidled her way to the lavatory.

Not sure what she expected, she was nonetheless disappointed by the cramped booth. "People actually have sex in here?" she mumbled. A glance in the mirror evoked a shocked groan. Her makeup had disappeared, except for mascara that rimmed her eyes. Her hair was a sky-high rat's nest of tangles. Miserable, she looked down at her dress and shuddered—nothing much she could do there.

After washing her face with cool water, she opened her makeup bag to repair as much damage as possible. At the last minute, she held up a perfume bottle and gave her dress a couple of squirts. Too late, she realized she'd only intensified the stench. Cursing under her breath, she exited the cubicle and made her way self-consciously back to her seat, aware of passengers recoiling in her wake.

Alan was still dozing when she lowered herself into the seat. The pounding in her head had lessened, making room for reality to ooze into the crevices of her brain. In her occupation, vacations were hard to come by because time off meant missed commissions on home deals that were possibly months in the making. She'd passed up a week in Jamaica with Nick the All-Nighter, and a long weekend in San Francisco with Delectable Dale.

Only to squander seven days in close, romantic quarters with Annoying Alan.

The captain's voice came over the intercom and announced they were beginning their final descent to Fort Myers. Beside her, Alan roused and started to smile, then his nostrils flared. "Oh my," he said, his eyes watering.

Pamela frowned sourly. "You're no fresh breeze yourself."

"A shower would feel pretty good right now," Alan agreed, then touched his forehead. "Not to mention a couple of aspirin. We really tied one on."

Pam nodded. "Tequila will make you say and do strange things." She caught his gaze and studied his eyes, wondering if he was having as many misgivings about his hasty invitation as she was about her impulsive acceptance.

But his ice-blue eyes gave away nothing. "Better buckle up," he said, pointing, then smiled shyly. "Need a hand?"

Inhaling sharply, she shook her head. She could handle the guys who thought they were macho, the self-assured lady-killers—they were safely shallow. What she couldn't handle was Alan's Mr. Nice Guy persona...it threw her off balance.

It was six-thirty when they emerged from the airport, and dusk appeared to be converging. With only a few wrong turns, they found the car rental where Alan's reservations had been made.

"I'm sorry, sir," the clerk said, smiling sympathetically. "We're all out of full-size luxury cars. We'll have to step you down—with a sizable discount, of course."

Alan sighed and pinched the bridge of his nose. "Okay, I'll take a midsize."

The man tapped on the keyboard, then made a clicking noise with his cheek. "No, sorry."

"Utility vehicle?"

More clicking. "Nada."

Alan pursed his lips. "What *do* you have available?"

The man smiled and pointed out the window to a row of tiny white compacts.

Alan shook his head firmly. "No way."

Pam frowned. He was exhibiting typical Parish behavior. "Alan," she whispered loudly. "What do you mean 'no way'? It's a lousy rental car—what do you expect?"

He looked at her and mirrored her frown. "The best."

She crossed her arms impatiently and tapped her foot. "I'm tired, sick and cranky—get the stupid car and let's go."

His mouth tightened in displeasure, but he nodded curtly to the clerk.

"*I'll* drive," Alan announced firmly a few minutes later as they approached the little car.

"Fine," Pamela said, not missing the dig. "I hope this resort is close by—I'm beat."

With a lot of cursing from Alan, and frustrated mutterings from Pam, they finally managed to wedge themselves into the car. Alan unfolded the map he'd purchased, taking up the entire interior of the car. "Looks like about a twenty-minute drive." Then he spent fourteen minutes rattling the map, trying to refold it.

Pam leaned her head back, forcing thoughts of the coming week from her mind. She'd just roll with the punches, as always. Why was she letting a few days with Alan rattle her? She was safe—the man wasn't the least bit attracted to her. But it was his uptight idiosyncrasies that were going to drive her crazy. He was still rattling that damned map. She reached over and tore it from his hands, wadded it into a ball and tossed it in the back seat. "Let's go."

ALAN SQUINTED at a sign as they drove by. "Did that sign say Penwrote or Pinron?"

"We're lost, aren't we?"

He scoffed and pushed up his glasses. "Of course not."

She sighed dramatically. "Oh, yeah, we're lost, all right."

"'Lost' is a relative term."

"And I guess you're one of those guys who'd rather run out of gas than stop and ask for directions."

"Well, if you hadn't destroyed the map—"

"Forget the map—pull off at the next exit."

Suddenly the car wobbled. At a thumping sound on the back right side of the car, he slowed. "Darn it," he mumbled as he steered the lame car to the shoulder of the road. "We've got a flat."

"Beautiful," Pam said, throwing her hands up in the air. "We're lost *and* we have a flat."

"Well, it's not my fault." He shoved the gearshift into park. "You're the one who insisted we take this, this…matchbox car to begin with!"

"So call them to bring us another car."

"My cell phone is in my suitcase in Savannah."

She reached into her purse and pulled out her own mobile phone, but frowned. "The battery's dead."

"Great. This is just great!"

She pointed down the highway. "There's probably a phone off that exit."

Exasperated, Alan said, "I'm sure there is, but by the time I've walked that far, I could have the tire changed."

She sighed mightily once more, then opened the passenger-side door and stepped out. Alan did the same and walked back to the tiny trunk, swaying as vehicles passed them at terrific speeds.

"Are you sure you know how to do this?" Pam asked suspiciously.

"Sure," he said with false confidence. He'd once read a roadside manual, and he was sure the information would come back to him. Men just knew these things, didn't they?

Thirty minutes later, he was on his back, still trying to position the jack, when he looked over to see Pamela standing with her skirt hiked up to her thighs, and her thumb jerked to the side.

"What the heck are you doing?" he shouted.

"Getting us a ride," she yelled matter-of-factly.

"Would you please cover yourself? You'll attract every serial killer in the vicinity."

"I don't care, as long as he'll give us a ride to the resort."

"I've almost got it," he lied.

"Sure," she said, unconvinced, then smiled wide into oncoming traffic.

He heard the sound of a large vehicle slowing down and glanced over to see a big rig edging onto the shoulder in front of their cracker-box car.

"It worked!" she squealed, trotting toward the truck.

Alan heaved himself to his feet and took off after her, grabbed her by the elbow and pulled her to a halt. "Are you crazy? Didn't your mother ever tell you not to accept rides from strangers?"

Pam angled her head at him. "Alan, there's no one stranger than you." Then she yanked her arm out of his grasp.

He frowned at the tire iron in his hand, then tested its weight and hurried after her. At least he could break the serial killer's knees if he tried anything funny.

The burly, bearded murderer was already climbing down from his rig, doffing his cap to his vivacious victim. The man hadn't yet noticed him, Alan observed.

"Howdy, little lady, having car trouble?"

He couldn't hear Pam's response, but from the tilt of her head, he assumed it was something pathetically feminine and appropriate. She did at least gesture back to Alan, and the man looked up at him, frowning at the tire iron in his hand. Alan swung it casually as he stepped up beside Pam, slapping the metal bar against his left palm as if he wielded the weapon often—and well.

"Name's Jack," the man said cautiously as he extended his grubby hand to Alan.

Alan sized him up. *Jack the Ripper, Jack the Jackal, Jugular Jack.*

Shifting the bar to his left hand, Alan firmly shook the paw the man offered, then spit on the ground in what he hoped was a universal he-man gesture.

"I'm Pamela and this is Alan," Pam said cloyingly, her eyes shining.

Jack looked them over. "You two just get married?"

"No," Alan said.

"Yes," Pam declared.

The trucker looked between them, and took a tentative step backward.

Pam shot Alan a desperate look. "I mean, yes," Alan said, conjuring up a laugh. He shrugged and winked at the man. "Still can't get used to the idea."

"We just need a ride," Pam said quickly. "To the..." She looked to Alan for help.

"The Pleasure Palisades," Alan said, somewhat self-consciously. Pam raised an eyebrow and he felt his neck grow warm.

Turning back to the man, she asked, "Do you know where it is?"

"Yeah," Jack said, tugging at his chin. "Y'all ever been there?"

"No," Alan said. "My secretary moonlights as a travel agent—she made all the arrangements. I hear it's a very nice place."

The trucker pursed his lips, then nodded slowly. "Yep."

"Can we get a ride?" Pam pressed. "We'll be glad to pay you for your trouble." She dug her elbow deep into Alan's rib. He gasped, then nodded.

"No bother," Jack said, turning to walk toward his truck. He swept his arm ahead of him. "Climb on in."

"What're you hauling?" Pam's new drawl and buoyant step were evidence she'd already bought into the little adventure.

"Hogs," the man said proudly as he climbed up to open the passenger-side door.

"Hogs?" Alan parroted as Pamela clambered inside. She was barefoot again, carrying her shoes in one hand.

"Yep." The man grinned as he waited for Alan to get in beside her. Still gripping the tire iron solidly, Alan glanced over his shoulder uneasily.

"You'll need to put down that tire iron, son," the man said bluntly.

Alan straightened and puffed out his chest. "And why is that?"

Another grin. "So you can hold Barbecue," the man said, pointing inside.

"Oh, it's a baby!" Pam cooed.

Letting down his guard slightly, Alan slid one eye toward the cab. Pamela was sprawled in the seat, leaning over to fondle a tiny pig on the floorboard.

"That's Barbecue," the man said, laughing. "Born a few days ago. The rest of the litter died, so I figured I'd keep him up here till the end of the run."

"He's adorable," Pam said, squealing as loudly as the nervous, quivering pig.

"Get in, son," Jack said, giving him a slight shove.

Alan spilled into the deep seat. The door banged closed behind him. "We're goners," he said to Pam.

Her forehead creased. "What?"

"The man's probably got all kinds of butcher tools on him, and a meat hook for each one of us."

"You're paranoid," she scoffed. "We're lucky he stopped."

Jack opened his door and climbed up behind the huge steering wheel, effectively halting their conversation. He pulled down the bill of his cap, then started the truck. It rumbled and coughed, then lurched into gear. "To the Pleasure Palisades," he crowed, slapping his knee. "You folks will have a dandy wedding night there."

Alan's heart pounded and he didn't dare look at Pam. He glanced at his watch and almost laughed out loud. Less than eight hours ago, he was ready to walk down the aisle to marry Jo Montgomery, hoping the act of commitment would put a new spin on their lackluster sex life. Instead he was sitting in the cab of a big pig rig with a woman who smelled almost as bad as the cargo, with only the promise of a lumpy sofa bed to sleep on—*if* they ever made it to the resort.

Pamela chatted with Jack, while Alan sank deeper into the seat. He felt moisture on his foot and looked down in time to see Barbecue squatting over his shoe. Alan didn't have the energy to pull away, so he simply lay his head back on the cracked vinyl. He'd officially sunk to the level of piglet pee post. What a poetic way to sum up the day.

3

"ARE YOU SURE this is it?" Pamela peered out the window at the four-story structure. Half of the sign's neon letters were unlit.

"Yep," Jack said.

"Linda said it was an older resort, but with a lot of atmosphere." Alan said, frowning slightly. "It's beach-front, though—I think I can see the water from here."

"Well, it's hard to tell much in the dark," Pam said agreeably, allowing Alan to help her down from the truck. His hands were strong around her waist, and he set her only a few inches in front of him. Surprised at her body's re-action, she quickly stepped back.

They looked up and waved to thank the trucker. Jack leaned out of his window and yelled, "Wish I were you tonight, son. She's a looker!"

Pleased, Pam grinned, then glanced at Alan. He'd turned beet red and his smile was tight as he nodded at the man, speechless. Pam felt sorry for Alan being put on the spot, so she scrambled for something to smooth over the mo-ment. "Well, let's get checked in. I can't wait to get out of these clothes."

Too late, she realized she'd only added fuel to the fire. Alan cleared his throat, then turned toward the entrance. Without the lights of the truck, the parking lot was plunged into darkness. She took a step, then stumbled and grabbed the back of his jacket on the way down, very nearly taking him with her. He straightened and reached for her, his hands moving over her in search of a handhold. She felt him latch on to her shoulder and heard the rip of fabric as he came up with a handful of chiffon ruffles. He cursed and pulled her to her feet with an impatient sigh. "Do you think we can manage the last hundred yards without another catastrophe?"

She nodded, shocked at the sensations his hands were causing. It was the alcohol, the hunger, the exhaustion, the darkness—all of it combined to play games with her mind. What she needed was rest and daylight to remind her he was only uptight, dweeby Alan.

He grasped her elbow and steered her in the direction of the hotel. Pam suddenly had a premonition about the place and the week to come, but she kept her mouth shut and tucked her torn ruffles inside her bodice.

Flanked on either side by two gigantic plastic palm trees, the front entrance was less than spectacular. A dank, musty smell rose to greet them when they stepped onto the faded orange carpet of the gloomy reception area. To their right, stiff vinyl furniture so old it was back in style and more plastic plants encircled a portable TV set with an impressive rabbit-ear antenna. A home shopping channel was on, and two polyester-clad, middle-aged couples sat riveted to the screen. To their left, the gift shop was having a clearance on all Elvis items. Pam pursed her lips—maybe she could expand her collection.

She glanced at Alan to gauge his reaction. He was frowning behind his glasses, clearly ready to bolt. "This isn't exactly what I expected," he mumbled. She bit down on her tongue, suddenly annoyed. She doubted if he'd ever spent a night in less than four-star accommodations.

The reception desk stood high and long in front of them, dwarfing the skinny frizzy-haired clerk behind the half glass. She was snapping a mouthful of chewing gum. "Can I help you?" she asked disinterestedly, not looking up. She was surrounded by cheap paneling and sickly colors. In a word, the decor was garish. Alan's ex-fiancée, an interior designer, would have fainted on the spot. Yet for Pam, the place had a certain...retro charm.

"Hello," Alan said tightly. "I'm not sure this is the right place. Are there any other hotels named Pleasure Palisades in the area?"

Twiggy glanced up, her eyes widening in appreciation as she scanned Alan. She completely ignored Pam. "Nope," she said, sounding infinitely more interested. "This is it."

Alan gave Pam a worried glance, then looked back to the clerk. "Do you have a reservation for Mr. and Mrs.—" He coughed, then continued. "For Parish?"

"Parish?" She flicked a permed hank of dark hair over her shoulder, turned to a dusty computer terminal and clicked her fingers over the keyboard. "Parish... Parish...yep, Mr. and Mrs. Alan P. Parish, the deluxe honeymoon suite through next Friday night." She glanced up and added, "With complimentary VCR and movie library since it's almost Valentine's Day."

Alan's eyes widened in alarm. "We're in the right place?" Twiggy didn't answer, only blew a huge pink bubble with the gum, sucked the whole wad back into her mouth, then smiled.

"I'm sure the room is nice," Pam whispered, trying to sound optimistic. As long as it had running water, she couldn't care less.

He held up his finger to the girl. "Just one moment." He curled his hand around Pam's upper arm and pulled her aside. "There must be some mistake. I'll call Linda and get this straightened out *immediately*. I saw a Hilton a couple miles down the road—we'll get a room there tonight."

Pam was shaking her head before he finished. "I don't have 'a couple miles' left in me or in these shoes." She stamped her foot for emphasis.

"We'll call a cab," he said, frowning.

She stabbed him in the chest with her index finger. "*You* call a cab, and *you* go down the road to the Hilton. I'm tired and I'm hungover. As long as this place is clean, I'm staying!"

He took a step back and poked at his glasses. "You don't have to get nasty about it."

She swept an arm down the front of her dress. "That's the point, Alan. I *am* nasty."

Holding up his hands, he relented. "Okay, okay—we'll stay one night."

Two minutes later, the clerk swiped his credit card, then handed them two large tarnished keys. "Room 410 in the corner, great view, cool balcony. But the elevator is out of order, so you'll need to take the stairs." She smiled tightly at Pam this time, and snapped her gum. "Have a pleasant stay."

Alan moved in the direction she indicated, but Pam grabbed his arm. "I'll need to purchase a few things to change into," she reminded him, nodding toward the gift shop.

"You need something in the gift shop?" the girl asked. She didn't wait for an answer, just reached under the counter and pulled out a piece of cardboard that read, "Back in a few," and propped it against a can of cola. "I'm the cashier, too." She snapped her gum and emerged from behind the wooden monstrosity.

Pam followed the girl into the gift cubbyhole, rubbing her tired eyes. "Alan, what does the 'P' stand for?" She quickly surveyed the dusty merchandise on the cramped shelves, searching for items to help her get through the week.

Alan moved to the other side of the store, intent on his own shopping. "What 'P'?"

She stacked toiletries in her arms, then moved to a wall rack of miscellaneous clothing. "Your middle initial, what does it stand for?"

He was silent for several seconds, then said, "Never mind."

She turned around and grinned, her curiosity piqued. "Come on, what's your middle name?"

The frown on his face deepened. "Forget it, okay?"

"Well, it has to be something odd or you wouldn't be so touchy."

He looked away.

"Parnell?"

"No."

"Purcell?"

"No."

"Prudell?"

"Pam." His gaze swung back to her, his voice low and menacing. "Don't."

She made a face at him, then turned her attention back to the shelves. She'd need shorts and a T-shirt, not to mention underwear. Pam spied a single package of men's cotton boxer shorts and picked it up, then stopped when she realized Alan also had a hand on them. They played a game of mini-tug-of-war, with each tug a little stronger than the last.

She yanked the package. "I didn't figure you for a boxer man, Alan."

He pulled harder. "And I didn't figure you for a boxer woman, Pam."

She jerked the package. "You don't know me very well."

"I *have* to have underwear," he protested, then nearly stumbled back when she abruptly released the package.

Pam acquiesced, palms up. "Since underwear has always been optional for me, they're all yours."

His Adam's apple bobbed and he looked contrite. "M-maybe we can share."

Perhaps it was the timbre of his voice, or his boyish, disheveled appearance, or Elvis's "Blue Christmas" playing softly in the background, but Pamela suddenly felt a pull toward Alan, and it scared her. "I don't think so," she said more haughtily than she meant to.

Alan shrugged. "Suit yourself. Do you have everything you need?"

Nodding, Pam yanked an Elvis T-shirt and a pair of pink cotton shorts off the rack, then heaved her bounty onto the counter.

Alan piled his items on top. "I'll get these things," he said, opening his wallet. She started to protest, but he held up his hand. "It's the least I can do," he said, then raised an eyebrow when the clerk lifted a package of rub-on tattoos from Pam's things.

Pam grinned. "I always wanted a tattoo."

Five minutes later she lifted her skirt, shifted her packages and tilted her head back to look up the stairwell that seemed to go on and on. She was exhausted and again her decision to share a room with Alan for a week seemed ludicrous. On the way up they had to stop several times to rest, then walked down a dimly lit outdoor walkway, past several doors to reach the last room, 410.

Pam could hear the ocean breaking on the beach below them, and she leaned over the railing to get a better look. Suddenly Alan's arm snaked around her waist and dragged her back against his chest. The length of his body molded to hers, and Pam gasped as her senses leaped. After a few seconds, he released her gently, then admonished in a low voice, "I don't trust that railing, and I don't want to make a trip to the hospital tonight."

Her heart still pounding in her chest, Pam laughed nervously and listened while he fidgeted with the key in the dark. "You'd think they could put up a few lights," Alan muttered. He pushed open the door, reached around the corner and flipped on a switch.

They stood and stared inside the room in astonishment.

"They obviously saved all the lights for the *interior*," he added flatly.

Pam nodded, speechless. The room's chandelier was a dazzling display of multicolored lights, multiplied dozens of times by the room's remarkable collection of mirrors.

"It's a disco," he mumbled.

And the bed was center stage. Huge and circular, it was raised two levels. A large spotlight over the padded headboard shone onto the satiny gold-colored comforter, and Pam doubted the light was meant for reading.

"At least the carpet is new," she said, stepping inside.

"Yeah," he said. "And I'm sure they paid top dollar—brown shag is really hard to find."

She glanced around the room, at the avocado-green kitchenette, the makeshift living room consisting of a battered sofa—presumably the pullout bed—and two chaise-size beanbag chairs. The sitting area was "separated" from the sleeping area by two short Oriental floor screens. The wide-screen TV was situated to be visible from the bed or from the sofa.

"It's spacious," she observed. "And functional."

"Yeah—for orgies."

She scoffed and set down her bags, crossing the room to

inspect the bed. She poked at the comforter and watched the bed ripple. "It's a water bed," she said, grinning. "And look." She held up a small bottle lying on the pillow. "Complimentary body liqueur—cinnamon." She twisted off the lid, then dipped her index finger in and tasted it. "Mmm, I'm starved."

Alan rolled his eyes, then looked around the room as if plotting how to get through the night without touching anything. "It's a dump," he pronounced.

Pam replaced the liqueur. It was a repeat of the car rental—nothing but the best was good enough for Alan Parish. "Lighten up, Alan, this is fun."

"Speak for yourself," he muttered, shaking his head.

Straightening, she put her hands on her hips and threw back her shoulders. "Why don't you come down from your high horse and see how the other half lives?"

"What the hell is that supposed to mean?"

"It means life isn't always first-class, and you have to learn to roll with the punches."

He squared his jaw. "I can roll with the best of them."

"Hah! You can't even *bend,* Alan, much less roll. You're just a spoiled little rich boy."

"I resent that," he said, his eyes narrowing.

"Go ahead—it's still the truth." She jerked up the bag that contained her new toiletries and headed in the direction of what appeared to be the bathroom. She opened the door, then breathed, "Wow."

A large red sunken tub dominated the room, appropriately set off by pale pink tile. It appeared that the sink, shower and commode had been miniaturized to make room for the tub, which could easily accommodate three adults.

"Hmm," Alan said behind her. "Another novelty." His voice was still laced with sarcasm.

"But not the last," Pam said, pointing out the picture window over the tub.

Their room was the last one set in a U formation, giving them a perfect view over an open plaza of the brightly lit room on the opposite side. Though not as spectacular as theirs, the room was furnished in the same style and occupied by an elderly couple who clearly had a disdain for clothing. Pam stared, fascinated, as the couple moved around in the kitchen, completely nude—with no tan lines. "It's like watching a car crash," she murmured. "You don't want to look, but you can't help yourself."

The woman turned her gaze directly toward them, then nudged her husband. Pam and Alan stood frozen, like two animals caught in headlights. Then the couple smiled and waved.

Alan reached forward and yanked the curtain closed over the tub. "Unbelievable," he muttered. "Those people are old enough to be my parents."

Pam leaned over and turned on the hot-water faucet. The first few trickles of water looked a little rusty, but it ran clear within a few seconds, so she stopped up the tub and poured in a handful of scented salts from a gold plastic container.

"Not everyone loses interest in sex when they get older, Alan." Then her best friend's comments about her drab intimate relationship with Alan rattled around in her head. "Assuming a person was ever interested in sex in the first place," she added dryly.

She reached around the back of her dress to capture the zipper in her fingers, and began to ease it downward. Suddenly, she remembered Alan was still in the room, and stopped. Holding up her neckline, she sighed. "Alan, I don't have the energy to throw you out, but I'm warning you—these clothes are coming off in the next few seconds, so if you don't want to be embarrassed twice in one evening, you better vamoose.''

He paled, then groped for the doorknob and bolted out of the room. Pam giggled, then slid the zipper down and escaped from the hideous, rancid dress. After ripping off her shredded panty hose, she unhooked her bra and stepped into the heavenly, hot bubbles.

"Ahhhh," she breathed, sinking in up to her neck. Leaning her head back, she closed her eyes, her hands moving over her body to dislodge the day's grime. She automatically lapsed into a series of isometric exercises she always performed in the tub or shower for toning and relaxing. After a few minutes, her limbs grew languid, but her skin tingled.

Gingerly, she lifted her head and looked toward the closed door. Scooping up a handful of bubbles, she trickled them across her raised leg. Alan Parish was the most conservative, stuffy man she'd ever met under the age of sixty. Of course, he did have a lot to live up to, being the oldest son of such a prominent Savannah family. A subdivision had even been named for them—Parish Corners. He was a regular pillar of the community, unlike herself, who had nowhere to go in the world but up.

And here they were, two opposing forces, thrown together in a tacky hotel room. Paper and matches. Roses and switches. Uptown and downtown.

She smiled wryly. Inviting her to come on the trip was no doubt the most spontaneous thing Alan had ever done in his life. How ironic that he was probably the only man in Savannah who would invite her to spend a week with him, without having anything sexual in mind. Pam eased her head back. She could relax—Alan Parish's relationship with her was even less than platonic.

ALAN PASSED A HAND over his face and paced the length of the room. He wouldn't have believed it possible to be so tired and yet so awake at the same time. His hungover head was screaming for sleep, but the rest of his body was rigidly aware that Pamela Kaminski, a woman who had a sexual position named for her—the Kaminski Curl—was in the next room, naked...and lathered.

He swore and ripped off his bow tie, then tossed it across the room. When he caught a glimpse of himself in one of the many mirrors, he came up short, surprised at the anger he saw in his face. He prided himself on always remaining calm, regardless of the situation, but today—he sighed and shoved his fingers through his hair—today he'd been put through the wringer by two different women. His laugh was short and bitter. If he didn't know better, he'd suspect it was a conspiracy.

His empty stomach rolled, prompting him to call the front desk. Twiggy's bored drawl was instantly recognizable. "Yeah?"

Alan bit back a tart comment, and instead mustered a pleasant tone. "My—uh, *our* package includes meals, and I was wondering if the hotel restaurant is still open."

"Just closed," she said cheerfully.

He groaned. "We're starved—can we get room service?"

Twiggy sighed dramatically. "What do you want?"

"A couple of steaks and a bottle of wine."

"I'll see what I can do."

"Thanks." He hung up and frowned sourly at the phone. How had his secretary found this place? Remembering he still needed to find accommodations for the rest of the week, he called Linda's voice mail and left her a message to call him. Then he contacted the car rental agency who promised to have another car delivered to their hotel first thing in the morning.

Trying mightily to forget the events of the last few hours, Alan removed the black studs from his buttons, shrugged out of his wrinkled shirt and folded it neatly over the back of a stiff kitchen chair. He slipped off his shoes and socks, then lowered himself to the dreadful carpet and performed fifty push-ups. Breathing heavily, he pulled himself to his feet, wincing at the odor of his own sweat. A shower before dinner would feel terrific. Glancing at his watch, he frowned and hesitated, then went to the bathroom door and rapped lightly. Steam curled out from under the door, warming his bare toes. Alan swallowed. "Pam?"

He heard her moving in the water, splashing lightly.

"I ordered room service and it should be here soon."

She didn't answer. Alan shifted from foot to foot, wondering if she'd fallen asleep in the water. Suddenly, the door swung open and Pam stood before him, holding the ends of a dingy white towel above her breasts, her hair dripping wet. His breath caught in his throat, and the room seemed to close in around them.

Pamela smiled benignly. "I left my new clothes out here," she said, pointing to a bag on the floor. She brushed by him, her clean, soapy scent rising to fill his nostrils. He watched with blatant admiration as she walked over to retrieve the articles. Her long, slender legs were glowing with bath oil and speckled with water. His heart skipped a beat when the towel sagged low enough in the back to expose her narrow waist and the top of her—

"Astringent," she mumbled, rummaging in the bag.

"Wh-what?" he croaked.

"Remind me to buy astringent tomorrow when we go shopping," she said, bending over, the towel inching up to reveal the backs of her thighs.

Alan felt his knees weaken, and averted his glance to the ceiling as he cleared his throat. "Okay." The plastic bag rattled.

"And a hair dryer."

"Sure." He sneaked another peek. Her back was still turned, and she was still standing butt up, the towel barely covering her. Squeezing his eyes shut, he suppressed a groan.

"Are you okay?"

His eyes snapped open. Pam was staring at him, squinting.

"Uh, tired and hungry, same as you, I suppose."

She nodded toward the bathroom. "You'll feel better once you shower." .

Gratefully, he escaped to the bathroom, where he leaned heavily against the closed door for a few seconds to compose himself. But he was still muttering to himself a few minutes later when he stepped under the cold spray of the cramped shower. Any other man would have ripped off that towel and carried Pam to the bed...so why hadn't he? Sighing, he massaged his tired neck muscles. Because Pam would have welcomed it from any other man. But he'd been around Pam enough to realize she saw him as little more than a big brother—completely asexual. Why else would she have sashayed into the room practically naked, as if he wasn't there? She hadn't acknowledged his masculinity enough even to be modest around him. It was downright insulting. Just because he wasn't like the Neanderthals she typically dated didn't mean he wasn't alive.

A tapping sound on the shower glass startled him. "Alan?"

He froze, then whirled, instinctively crossing his hands over his privates.

4

PAM BLINKED. She'd seen so-so bodies and she'd seen good bodies. But who would have thought this magnificent specimen had been walking around Savannah all this time disguised as Alan Parish? Wide, muscled shoulders, smooth chest, washboard stomach...now if only he'd move his damn hands out of the way.

Through the steamed glass of the shower door, his face was screwed up in anger. "Pam!" he yelled. "Do you just walk in on a person no matter what they're doing?"

Pam gave him a wry smile. "Don't get your bowels all twisted, Alan. Unless yours is green, you don't have anything I haven't seen before. Your secretary is on the phone."

"Linda?" he asked, talking above the noise of the water.

"How many secretaries do you have?"

"Has she found another place for me—us—to stay?"

Pam sighed impatiently. "I didn't ask, Alan. I think she's still recovering from the fact that a woman answered the phone."

His eyes widened. "Did you think to disguise your voice?"

She planted her hands on her hips in annoyance. "Sorry, I was fresh out of helium, but I think we're safe."

Alan nodded, the water streaming down his face. "You're probably right—she'd never suspect you were here with me."

"No one would," Pamela agreed dryly. "Not in a million years."

He stared at her, nodding and dripping, then sputtered, "Well?"

"Well, what?"

"Well, hand me a towel!"

Pam grinned, enjoying his self-consciousness, then reached for the remaining bath towel folded not so neatly on the toilet tank. She dangled the flimsy cloth in front of the shower door and watched as he considered uncovering himself to retrieve it. Thirty seconds passed.

Alan shifted and blushed deep pink. "Just drape it over the top of the stall, will you?"

Pressing her lips together to control her smirk, Pam tossed the towel over the top of the shower door and Alan grabbed it just as it passed his waist. She laughed and exited the room shaking her head.

Imagine, she thought as she collapsed on a yellow beanbag chair and began to untangle her wet hair, Alan was *modest.* It was actually kind of…refreshing in an attractive man, quite the opposite from the chest-pounding antics of her transient lovers. Then she frowned. Maybe Alan was more than just a "lights off" kind of guy—maybe he harbored a host of hang-ups that kept him from enjoying sex. Her friend Jo had never gone into specifics, and even though Pam had been dying to know details, she'd respected her friend's privacy.

The sound of the bathroom door opening broke into her thoughts. Alan emerged in a pair of navy sweatpants and strode over to the phone. He was polishing his glasses with the bath towel and didn't look at her, but the set of his shoulders told her he was still ruffled by her invasion. He shoved aside the wet hair hanging in his eyes, yanked up the handset and turned his back to Pam.

"Hello, Linda?"

Unabashed, Pam used the opportunity to more closely scrutinize his startling physique. His skin was damp and glowing, golden and sleek, like a swimmer's.

"You just got back from the wedding? They must have had a blowout reception."

His shoulders were wide and covered with knotty muscle that rolled under his skin as he paced around the nightstand, gripping the phone.

"No, Linda, don't feel bad—I'm glad you enjoyed the champagne...well, thanks for the condolences, but it's probably for the best."

She could smell the clean, soapy scent of him even at this distance, stirred up every time he pivoted on his bare feet.

"Yeah, I decided to take the trip anyway."

Pam squinted at the length and width of his feet, made a few mental calculations, then pursed her lips in admiration.

"Let's just say this place is not exactly what I expected."

The baggy sweatpants dipped low to reveal the top of his hard-won boxers and a narrow waist. Being a computer nerd must be more physically demanding than she thought.

"Actually, Linda, it's a dump."

Now that she thought of it, she *had* passed him going in and out of the workout club a couple of times.

"What do you mean, this is the only room available?"

His butt was narrow and hard, like a greyhound's... aerodynamic...built for speed. Desire struck low in her abdomen, shocking her.

"The woman who answered?" Alan glanced at her over his shoulder, then quickly back to the phone. "Uh, nobody…that is…nobody you'd know.'' He laughed nervously. ''A m-maid.''

Pam frowned, but a knock at their door and thoughts of food distracted her. She scrambled up and swung open the door, then practically snatched the covered food tray from Twiggy's hands. When the girl stuck out her skinny foot to prevent Pam from shutting the door, Pam smirked, set down the tray and shoved a five-dollar bill into her bony hand.

She slammed the door with a bang and motioned for Alan to get off the phone. He nodded, his face a mask of frustration. ''Just keep checking, Linda, and let me know when you find something.''

By the time he hung up, Pam was already sitting crosslegged on the water bed and lifting the lid from their meal.

''Bad news.'' He sat on the edge of the mattress and triggered a small tidal wave.

''I know—no pickles,'' Pam said, staring down at a platter of grilled-cheese sandwiches.

''Linda says it's the height of the season, and with Valentine's Day only a few days away, everything is booked.''

''Damn,'' she mumbled, sinking her teeth resignedly into the surprisingly good sandwich. ''I really wanted pickles.''

''She's going to call if something opens up.''

''Mmphh,'' Pam said, licking gooey orange cheese from her finger.

Alan stared at the food tray. ''I ordered steak. That is not steak.''

''But it's good,'' she mumbled, cracking open a can of cold soda.

''And that is definitely not wine.''

She glanced up at him. ''You ordered wine?''

He blushed, then stammered. ''W-well, you know, the meals are already paid for.''

"I thought I was too tired to eat, but I was wrong." She stuffed in the last bite of her sandwich.

Alan picked up a sandwich by the corner and sniffed it. "Cholesterol city."

"My hometown," Pam said with a smile, then she tore off a huge chunk of a second greasy sandwich. "Live a little, Alan."

He wrinkled his nose and took a tentative bite, then chewed slowly. "Linda said the wedding was a big hit."

At the serious tone of his voice, Pam stopped munching and searched for something comforting to say, but nothing came to mind.

"I thought Jo really loved me," Alan said without self-pity. He seemed genuinely perplexed.

"She did," Pam quickly assured him. "She told me so many times."

"Then she fooled us both."

Pam shook her head, then finger-combed her wet bangs. "That's not true—Jo doesn't have a deceitful bone in her body. Look how close she came to marrying you because she thought it was the right thing to do."

Alan gave her a wry smile. "Pam, don't ever go into motivational speaking."

"Okay, that didn't come out just right, but you get the gist—she really does care about hurting you."

His blue eyes darkened. "I knew John Sterling was trouble the minute I laid eyes on him."

Pam chose her words carefully. "It takes two to tango, Alan." Then she muttered to herself, "Three in France."

He sighed heavily. "You're right. She certainly fell hard for him."

Sympathy barbed through Pam—the man *had* been robbed of the future he'd planned. She felt compelled to say something. "Well, if you ask me, Jo missed out." Pam leaned sideways to give Alan's shoulders a friendly squeeze, but she was unprepared for the electricity beneath her fingers when she made contact with his smooth skin. Alan jerked his head around and their faces were mere inches apart.

For a few seconds, neither one spoke. Pam swallowed audibly.

"Do you really think she missed out?" Alan asked, his voice barely above a whisper, his gaze locked with hers.

Sirens went off in Pam's head. She fought the waves of awareness that flooded her—his scent, his warmth, his incredible physique. Her body softened and hardened in response. Sexual energy flamed to the surface and singed the fringes of her mind. Incredibly, a message was delivered to her brain amidst the smoke and fire. *It's Alan. Alan—who's still in love with your best friend.*

Pam inhaled sharply and pulled back carefully, not wanting to make the moment even more awkward. The fluid mattress bumped them up and down. She laughed nervously. "Yeah, I do," she said brightly, then swept her arm out toward the room. "She missed all of this on her wedding night."

To her relief, Alan smiled and looked around. "Something tells me she wouldn't have appreciated all this, um, atmosphere as much as you do. Jo would never have climbed into that ridiculous tub."

"It was fun."

"And she would never have sat on a beanbag chair."

"The most underrated furniture on the market, in my opinion."

"And this bed..." He laughed, smacking the shiny comforter, then bobbing up and down with the waves. "She would *never*—" He stopped midlaugh and glanced up, then blushed.

Pam grinned and shrugged. "She might have surprised you. Water beds aren't so bad."

With one eyebrow raised, Alan reached for another sandwich. "You speak from experience, I take it."

She nodded amiably. "My first experience, as a matter of fact. Which was so unremarkable, it's a wonder I don't have a bad association with water beds."

He laughed again. "My first time was less than memorable, too. To this day I have an aversion to spiral stairs."

Surprise shot through her, and she couldn't keep it out of her voice. "Spiral stairs? *You*, Alan?"

His smile was sheepish. "I seem to remember that was also my first introduction to Kentucky bourbon."

"Ah," she said knowingly. "Been there, done that." She dropped her half-eaten cheese sandwich onto the platter and stifled a huge yawn. "I think the day is catching up with me, but it's scarcely ten-thirty."

He glanced toward the television cabinet. "How about a movie before we, um, turn in?"

"Sure," she said, shifting on the bed, flashing forward to their sleeping arrangements. She felt restless and uncomfortable with her newfound attraction to Alan, and grateful he didn't share her momentary indiscriminate horniness. But the thought of sleeping with Alan and then returning to Savannah to face her friend Jo was enough to have her begging her guardian angel for strength.

She watched out of the corner of her eye as Alan removed the food tray and slid it onto the dresser. He moved with casual elegance, running a hand through his drying hair, separating the glossy strands. Pam groaned and crossed her arms over her saluting breasts, squeezed her eyes shut and whispered, "Oh Holy Angel, forsake me not..."

At the sound of his moan, she peeked. Alan leaned over

and arched his back, cracking and popping the stretched vertebrae, flexing his well-toned upper body. Sweat broke out on her upper lip. "...give no place to the evil demon to subdue me..."

"I hope this free video library has something decent to offer." He straightened, then walked over to the cabinet and swung open the door. When he knelt down to finger the row of black video cases, his baggy sweatpants inched even lower, revealing more of the new pale blue boxers.

"...take me by my wretched and outstretched hand..."

"Oh, great," he scoffed, his back to her. "*Denise Does Denver, Long, Dark, and Lonesome,* and the soon-to-be-classic *Tripod Man.*"

"...and keep me from the front—I mean, every affront of the enemy..."

"Did you say something, Pam?"

Her eyes widened. Alan was squinting back at her over his shoulder. She straightened and smiled, her mind racing. "N-no, just reciting my to-do list for tomorrow."

He frowned. "To go shopping?"

"No, I, uh...I have a big home deal in the works that I have to check on." Which was the absolute truth, although she hadn't given it any thought until now.

"Anyplace I'd know?"

"The Sheridan house."

He whistled low. "That should be quite a commission."

"That's why I need to check on it."

After reshelving the tapes, he retrieved the remote control and pushed himself up from the floor to sit at the foot of the bed. With his back to her still, he asked, "Isn't the Sheridan house haunted?"

Pam felt the wave he'd started ripple beneath her rear end. "*Please* don't add fuel to that rumor—the house has been on the market for nearly two years and I finally have an interested buyer." *And please don't come any closer.*

"Hey—'X-Files' reruns." He turned and clambered up to join her on the bed, a happy grin on his face. After stacking the slippery, bumpy pillows behind his back, he scratched his bare, flat stomach and crossed his long legs at the ankles.

Pam held her breath, rattled by his nearness. Her head bobbed from the rolling mattress. "I've seen this episode," she said, exhaling.

He turned his head toward her and pushed his glasses higher on his nose. "Really? You like this show?"

"Never miss it—I'm a big science-fiction fan."

His eyebrows rose. "Me, too."

Pam sat perfectly still, her thigh a mere eight inches from Alan's elbow. "So; do you think Mulder and Scully will ever get together?"

Alan made a clicking sound with his cheek and shook his head, his fair hair splaying against the shiny gold pillows. "I hope not."

"Why?"

"Because they're great just the way they are. Sex would...would—" He waved vaguely into the air. "Well, you know—"

"Complicate things," Pam offered, trying to relax.

He nodded. "Cloud the picture."

"Muddy the waters."

"Yeah, I'd hate to see them backslide to the 'X-*rated* Files.'" Alan smiled and forced himself to take his eyes off Pam and concentrate on the television show. His skin tingled from her proximity and he had to keep his leg bent in order to hide the other physical reaction she provoked. "Of course it's obvious that Mulder thinks Scully is really hot."

"You think?"

"Sure," he said, sneaking another peek up at her from his reclined position. He was eye level with her chest...and she wasn't wearing a bra. She glanced down at him, twisting a lock of dark blond hair around her finger. His bent leg began to tremble. "Can't you tell by the way he, um, looks at her all the time?"

She squinted at the screen. "Does he?"

"Yeah, and haven't you noticed that they're always invading each other's personal space?"

"How can you tell?"

"Eighteen inches. Americans like to keep a private space of eighteen inches around them." He started to draw an imaginary arc around him, but stopped when he realized the line would encompass Pam. His leg was practically jerking now. "Th-that space is reserved for, uh—"

"Intimacy?" she prompted, looking completely innocent.

His pulse leaped. "Or k-keyboards," he croaked.

Her finely arched eyebrows drew together. "What?"

He shrugged, suddenly feeling foolish. "Computer humor—most of us spend more time with our PC's than with any one person."

"Agreed—more than with any *one* person," she said, smiling wryly, then breaking out in a huge yawn.

Great, Parish. Not only is your conversation putting her to sleep, but you come off looking like some kind of freak who's turned on by his mainframe. And he hadn't missed her unnecessary reminder that when it came to sex, she liked to experiment. Which was an even bigger slap in the face considering they were in bed together and she was fighting to keep her eyes open.

He turned his attention back to the television, trying to lose himself in the fantasy on the screen. His wedding night was turning out to be somewhat less exciting than he'd hoped for. Not that he'd invited Pam along as a substitute for Jo—sleeping with her hadn't entered his mind.

Well, okay, so it *had* entered his mind, but not seriously. Not any more than when he saw a gorgeous model or movie star on TV. To him, Pamela had always seemed just as distant, just as untouchable. And even though the long expanse of her bare leg beckoned to him just a few inches away, she might as well have been still in Savannah for all the good it would do him.

He bit the inside of his cheek, his frustration mounting. One half roll of his body would put him face-to-breast with the most beautiful, sexual woman he knew. Maybe all he needed to do was make the first move. Maybe she'd rip off her clothes and he'd get to see what half of Savannah was raving about. Maybe they'd be great together and he'd give her a blinding orgasm.

His confidence surged, and he made a split-second decision. For once in his life, he would seize the moment and let the chips fall where they might. Before he could change his mind, he drew a quick breath and rolled onto his side, realizing the instant his chin met soft, pliant skin that he'd underestimated the distance *and* the size of her breasts. Her light floral scent filled his lungs, and his mind spun. His eyes darted to her face as he scrambled to think of something witty to say. Panic exploded in his chest...until he saw that she was sleeping.

He pulled himself up and expelled a small, disappointed sigh as he studied her lash-shadowed cheeks and the eternal pout of her fuller upper lip. He allowed his gaze to rove over her slender neck, then down to her breasts. The dark crescents of her nipples were barely visible beneath the thin fabric of her T-shirt. Elvis smiled at him, obviously happy to be stretched over Pam's ample bosom.

Alan's body hardened and he fought back a groan. He lifted his free hand and let it hover over an area where her shirt had risen high on her thigh. Was she wearing panties? Did he dare peek? After all, she'd seen him all but buck naked.

No, he decided. He wasn't a voyeur—he wanted anything that transpired between them to be consensual. "Pam," he whispered, his voice scratchy.

She moaned and moved down on the pillows and slightly toward him, but didn't rouse.

"Pam," he repeated a little louder.

He held his breath as her eyelashes fluttered for a second and her mouth opened as if she was going to speak. His desire for her swelled even more and his heart thumped in anticipation.

"Alan?" she murmured, her eyes still closed.

"Y-yes?" he whispered hopefully.

She wet her lips, and he thought he might go mad with wanting her. He moved toward her open mouth, intending to kiss her awake, but the sound emerging from her throat stopped him cold.

She was snoring…loud enough to shake the mirror on the ceiling above them.

5

PAM'S LEG itched. Trying to ignore it, she floated deeper into the pillow, enjoying the last fuzzy minutes of sleep. But the itch persisted until at last she reached down and scratched her knee vigorously. The thought that she needed to shave skittered across her mind, but was obliterated when she realized she hadn't even felt her fingernails against her skin.

Her eyes flew open, and she froze at the image in the mirror ceiling. Alan, stripped down to his boxers, lay wrapped around her like a koala bear in a eucalyptus tree, his arm resting comfortably across her chest, his bent leg heavy upon her abdomen. She could feel his warm breath upon the side of her neck. Her mind spun and panic welled within her. The last thing she remembered was watching television—had she…did they…oh, God, what was that stabbing into her side?

She pushed at his arm, dragging him with her as she attempted to roll away from his body. The fluid mattress surged, grabbed her, then slammed their bodies back together, abruptly rousing Alan from his slumber.

"Huh?" he muttered, lifting his head.

His glasses sat askew on the top of his head and his hair had finished drying in every direction but down. "Get off of me," Pam said, enunciating clearly.

Squinting, he appeared not to have heard her. "Alan," she repeated more loudly. "I'm not Jo—get off of me."

She knew the precise second her words registered because he stiffened and his nearsighted eyes rounded. "Pam?"

Throwing him a smile as dry as her mouth, she said, "Afraid so."

He wasted no time disentangling himself from her, but floundered a few seconds before propelling himself off the bed. Pam followed him with her eyes, averting her glance from the bulge straining at the front of his underwear. To avoid aggravating her mushrooming headache, she lay still until the waves stopped.

Patting furniture surfaces, presumably searching for his glasses, Alan walked into the half-unfolded sofa bed. Flesh collided with metal in a sickening thunk. "Son of a—" He broke off and bit his lower lip, wincing.

"They're on the top of your head, Einstein."

Alan fumbled for his glasses, jammed them on and looked back to the bed as if he still hadn't seized the situation.

She lifted her hand and fluttered her fingers at him. "I trust you slept well," she said in a sarcastic tone.

Patting down his hair, he scowled and bent over to scoop up his sweatpants. "How could I, with you snoring loud enough to rattle my teeth?"

Annoyance bolted through her, and she shot up, grimacing at the pain exploding in her temples. "Do you always curl into a fetal position when you're in agony? Our deal was *you* would sleep on the sofa bed!"

He reached down to massage his shin. "I tried to pry open the damn thing, but it wouldn't budge."

She rubbed her forehead, glancing around the sunlit room. "What time is it?"

He held the sweatpants in front of his waist with one

hand and picked up his watch with the other. "Almost ten o'clock."

She sighed, pushing tangled hair out of her eyes. "At least the stores should open soon."

"Forget the stores, give me a restaurant."

"Fine. We'll have a bite to eat, then I can go shopping." Thankfully, the awkwardness was dissolving. "Wonder what the weather will be like this week?"

Alan picked up the remote and found the weather channel, then tossed the control on the bed. Without another word, he turned and limped into the bathroom.

Pam frowned after him. He didn't have to be so snotty—after all, *he* had invited *her*. He wasn't being a very gracious host.

Oh, well, at least Mother Nature was smiling on them. According to the chipper weatherwoman, they had arrived smack in the middle of a February heat wave: temperatures in the low nineties, and sun, sun, sun.

Pam gingerly pulled herself out of bed and walked to the far end of the room, away from the bathroom. In the light of day, the kaleidoscope room really was horrid. Groaning, she reached overhead in a full-body stretch, wriggling her toes in the chocolate shag carpet, then drew aside the yellow brocade curtain covering a sliding glass door. The balcony Twiggy promised was a tiny wooden structure about the size of a refrigerator enclosed by worn railings. Despite the slight pain caused by the morning sunlight, she unlatched the door and stepped out into the cool air, feeling her spirits rise along with the gooseflesh on her arms.

A set of questionable-looking narrow stairs descended to a pebbly path that disappeared into palm trees and sea grass. She took a step forward, then stopped, rubbed one bare foot over the other, and decided not to chance it. If she fell and broke a leg, Alan might shoot her to put her out of his misery.

Without the wide sign from the neighboring Grand Sands Hotel, they might have had a very good view. Despite the obstruction, a slice of the white beach was visible, dotted with morning walkers and shell-seekers. The air, full of sand and salt dust, blew sharp against her bare arms and legs. Inhaling deeply, she drew in the tangy ocean breeze and was suddenly very glad she had come. Maybe the circumstances weren't ideal, but she loved the ocean and Savannah's beaches were a bit too cold to enjoy this time of year.

Humming to herself, she turned and reentered the room, closing the sliding door behind her. Then her gaze landed on the bathroom door and her smile evaporated. Obviously, Alan already regretted the invitation to share his honeymoon. She was a poor replacement for the woman he loved. But she was here, and she'd promised Jo she'd keep an eye on him. She blushed guiltily—the amount of time she'd spent eyeing him since their arrival probably wasn't what her friend had had in mind. Lifting her chin, she gathered her willpower. She could keep her lust at bay for a lousy week, but darn it, she wasn't going to let him mope and ruin the only vacation she'd had in over a year!

She took in her appearance in one of the many mirrors at her disposal and groaned out loud. As if he'd be interested, anyway. Her friend Jo rolled out of bed looking great. She, on the other hand, looked as if she'd been dragged backward through a hedgerow.

Dropping onto the unmade bed, she grabbed the phone. She needed to check her messages and see if old Mrs. Wingate had made up her mind about buying the Sheridan house, haunts and all. She retrieved her answering service with a few punched buttons. The message from Nick the

All-Nighter was wicked enough to fry the phone lines. And Jo had called, concern in her voice—had Pam seen Alan and was he all right?

She shot a look toward the bathroom door just as it opened. *Speak of the devil.* Swallowing, she scanned the tempting length of Alan in black running shorts and a tight touristy sweatshirt. He offered her a small smile, apparently in a much better mood. She lifted her finger, then turned away from him and tried to concentrate on Jo's rambling, heartfelt message. With a sigh, Jo thanked Pam for going after Alan and asked Pam to call her at John's house—Jo laughed—make that *her* house. Pam smirked into the phone, happy for her friend, but disturbed by the sticky mess she'd left behind.

She felt contrite as she replaced the handset. It wasn't Jo's fault that she was having these inappropriate feelings for Alan. "Jo left me a message."

Alan's handsome face remained impassive—perhaps a little *too* nonchalant. "What did she say?"

Pam hesitated, then said, "She was wondering if I'd seen you and how you're doing."

He exhaled loudly and cracked his knuckles in one quick movement. "What business is it of hers?"

"She's just worried about you—"

"Well, I'm not suicidal," he snapped.

Pam stood, jamming her hands on her hips. "You don't have to shoot the messenger."

"Sorry—I'm not feeling very well."

"Join the crowd," Pam yelled back, then touched a hand to her resurrected headache.

His expression softened a bit. "You don't look too bad—I mean, uh, you look…fine."

She smiled wryly, then turned toward the bathroom. "Nice try. I'll be out in two shakes."

Alan watched her retreat into the bathroom, the curves of her hips tugging at the hem of her T-shirt. A little more than *two* shakes, he amended silently, making fists of frustration at his side.

"This is insane," he said to the frantic-looking man in the mirror.

"Why are you worried about it?" his image asked. "Just *bed* the woman, for heaven's sake."

"I can't—she's my ex-fiancée's best friend."

"Even better."

Alan squeezed his eyes shut and cursed, then slowly opened them to address his argumentative reflection. "This is a fine mess you've gotten us into." Oh, well, maybe his secretary would come through with less evocative accommodations.

True to her word, Pam showered quickly, emerging like a ray of sunshine, her skin glowing, her golden hair caught up in a high, swishy ponytail. He groaned inwardly. She was even gorgeous in running shorts and a baggy white jersey sporting a multicolored parrot. "Ready?" she asked.

"And willing," he mumbled, picking up his wallet.

At the last minute, they both shoved their feet into hard, ill-fitting plastic thongs, then stumbled downstairs to find the reservation desk deserted. A fiftyish woman sprawled in one of the lobby chairs, smoking a long cigarette and watching a church program on television. She was happy to nod in the direction of the restaurant, and as soon as they smelled food their clumsy steps quickened.

Alan's stomach rumbled when he saw how packed the restaurant was. Grasping Pam's elbow, he pointed to the buffet line. "If you'll get us something to eat, I'll try to find a table." She nodded and he cased the area, his eyes lighting on a family of four wiping their chins over emptied plates. He scrambled toward the table, arriving at the same time as a busboy and an older couple holding laden plates.

The silver-haired man smiled. "Share?"

"Sure," Alan agreed.

"We're the Kessingers," the man supplied. "I'm Cheek and this is Lila."

Alan introduced himself as he pulled out the older woman's chair. "Another person will be joining me."

"We're from Michigan," Lila offered.

"Savannah," Alan told her, as he took a seat opposite her. The Kessingers seemed nice enough, divulging they were devoted snowbirds who migrated south every January until spring.

"There you are," Pam said, precariously balancing two plates piled high with food. Alan relieved her of half her burden, then introduced the senior couple.

"Hi," Pam said cordially as she swung into her seat.

Alan frowned down at the plate in front of him. Every single item was fried. "I see you got plenty of the *brown* food group."

"Eat," Pam said pointedly, stabbing a sausage patty with her fork.

With visions of whole-wheat bagels and fresh fruit dancing in his head, Alan ate, stopping frequently to sop the grease from his food with paper napkins. Lila Kessinger proved to be quite chatty, which gave Cheek plenty of time to ogle Pam, he noticed, surprised at the needle of jealousy that poked him.

"Are you newlyweds?" Lila asked.

Pam glanced at him. "No, we're just...uh..."

Alan's stomach fluttered. "Buddies," he offered.

"Pals," Pam affirmed.

"Oh," the woman responded. "I assumed you were married since you're in the honeymoon suite."

Alan stopped. "How did you know we're in the honeymoon suite?"

Lila grinned. "We're right across the plaza from you, in room 400. Remember—we waved."

He frowned, trying to recall, then grunted as Pam kicked him under the table. One look at her raised eyebrows and his memory flooded back. The naked couple! He dropped his fork with a clatter and a burning flush crept up his neck. "Oh, I didn't recognize you—"

"Because we're both nearsighted," Pam cut in. "We couldn't see much." She looked at him for reinforcement. "Isn't that right, Alan?"

"Y-yes," he said, a picture of the wrinkled nude couple emblazoned on his mind. "In fact, we didn't see anything at all. You waved, did you say?" He brought a glass of room-temperature water to his mouth for a drink.

Lila beamed and nodded. Cheek leaned forward, his eyes devouring Pam.

Lifting his wrist, Alan pretended to be shocked. "*Look* at the time. We have to go," he said, eyeing Pam.

"But I'm not finished," she protested.

"We'll get a stick of butter for the road," he said through clenched teeth, casting his eyes toward the door.

"Okay," she relented sullenly, wiping her mouth and standing. "It was nice to meet—"

Alan pulled on her arm, and nearly dragged her back through the restaurant.

"Let go of me," she said angrily, then jerked away from him. "What the devil is wrong with you?"

He stared at her and exclaimed, his frustration high, "That's the thanks I get?"

"Thanks? For what?"

"That dirty old man looked like he was getting ready to have *you* for breakfast!"

Pam tilted her head and laughed. "You're jealous!"

"What?" Alan scoffed, embarrassment thickening his tongue. "That'z we—ridiculous!"

"Weally?" Pam teased.

Grunting, Alan sputtered, "I thought you wanted to go shopping."

She grinned, looking triumphant. "I do."

"Then let's go see what the car rental agency delivered." He pivoted as quickly as the stupid sandals would allow, then flapped back toward the lobby, fuming. Damn, he hated her teasing, filing him in the same category as her bevy of besotted suitors.

Twiggy had returned to her post, and looked as bored as usual when he asked about the car. Without a word, she held up a key and pointed to the parking lot.

"Finally," he breathed, taking the key. "*Something* is going right."

He walked stiffly across the lobby and out into the parking lot, unable to look at Pam, still smarting from her taunt. He knew she was behind him, but he didn't know how close until he spotted their car, stopped dead in his tracks and felt her body slam into his.

"What's wrong?" she asked, stepping up beside him. Then she gasped. "A limo?" She whooped, then laughed until her knees buckled.

Alan, however, did not share her mirth. "This is unbelievable." He removed the letter tucked under the windshield wiper and read aloud. "Dear Mr. Parish, please accept this upgrade vehicle as our apology for your unfortunate breakdown—" He broke off and glanced at the powder blue stretch limousine. "They sent me a damn pimpmobile!"

Pam laughed even louder, clapping her hands. "What a blast!"

He stood paralyzed in shock as she swung open the back door. "Ooooh," she breathed, her eyes shining. "A television and everything!"

I'm in the twilight zone. "We're taking it back."

Her head jerked around. "What? We can't!"

"Oh, but we can."

Pam's eyebrows crumpled, and she pulled out her secret weapon: the pout. Damn! Surely she knew what that mouth did to him. He wavered. "Maybe we'll keep it just for the day."

She brightened and tumbled inside, then stuck her head back out. "I'll ride in the back." He felt the vacuum of air as she slammed the door.

Feeling like a colossal fool, he glanced around, opened the front door and slid behind the wheel. Pam had already found the button that operated the divider between them and was zooming the panel up and down.

"This is amazing," she squealed.

He glanced in the rearview mirror at her smiling face, watched her pressing buttons and exploring, and felt a strange tug at his heart. As exasperating as she could be, Pam's unflagging enthusiasm was undeniably charming. Somewhere between childhood and yuppiehood, he'd lost his zest for simple things...now he wondered how many wonderfully pure pleasures he'd overlooked the last several years.

"There's a refrigerator!" she exclaimed. "And olives!"

He pulled onto the highway, keeping one eye on Pam. She reclined in the back seat, propping her long legs on the bench seat running up the side. Then she unscrewed the lid from a slender jar and popped green olives into her mouth like a squirrel eating nuts. For some reason, he found the whole scene provocative.

"Hey, Alan, have you ever gotten naked in a limo?"

He weaved across the centerline so far he might have hit the oncoming car if the guy hadn't blared his horn and punctuated it with a hand gesture.

Breathing deeply to stem the charge of adrenaline through his body, he said, "I, uh, no, I can't say I have."

"Me neither."

Although her admission surprised him, he didn't say so. For a fraction of an instant, he entertained the idea of sharing Pamela's first sexual *something*. The way he figured it, the only new variable he could possibly add to her experience equation was location. Shaking the thought from his mind, he kept his dry mouth shut and his eyes peeled for signs indicating a mall.

Once he found a shopping center, it took several minutes to find a place to park. At last they were inside the mall and Alan felt some sort of normalcy returning at the sight of regular people in smart, upscale surroundings. He made a beeline for a well-known department store. "We can split up," Pam suggested.

Alan shook his head. "I'll go with you, I'm paying."

"Wait a minute—"

"Don't argue. I talked you into coming, and it's my responsibility—"

"I can take care of myself!"

He drew back at the change in her mood, the vehemence in her voice. He'd obviously hit a nerve, so he gentled his tone. "I know you can take care of yourself, Pam, but I'd feel bad if you spent money on top of taking time from your job. Let me do this—make me feel good." Immediately, he felt his skin warm at the implication of his own words.

She chewed on her lower lip, considering his words, then smiled slyly. "I think this may be the first time a guy has offered to do something for *me* to make himself feel good."

Glad her mood had lightened, he crossed his arms and mirrored her smile. "Maybe you've been hanging around with the wrong guys."

Her smile dissolved and her gaze locked with his. "Maybe you're right," she said, her voice barely above a whisper.

Alan studied her face and inhaled slowly, sure his chest was going to explode. This woman was driving him crazy. One minute she made him feel like an inept teenager, the next minute she made him feel as if he wanted to take care of her. Which was nuts because she'd made it perfectly clear she intended to take care of herself.

His fingers curled tighter around his biceps, itching to smooth the stray lock of hair back from her soft cheek. To hold her pointed chin and tilt her porcelainlike face up to the sun. To kiss that lopsided, upside-down, top-heavy pink mouth.

"Okay, go ahead," she said, shrugging.

He actually took a half step toward her before he realized she was talking about the clothing tab. "Where to first?"

"Men's shoes."

"What?"

She pointed to his red, thong-pinched feet and grinned. "You're going to need comfortable shoes to keep up with me."

Good idea, he decided three hours later as he shared a bench with an older gentleman outside the women's dressing room.

"Birthday?" the guy asked, obviously bored.

"No."

"Anniversary?" The man tapped out a cigarette and put it in his mouth, unlit.

"Uh-uh."

"Ah—you're in the doghouse."

"Well, not really."

"Oh, God," the man said, rolling his eyes. "Don't tell me you love her."

"Pam," he said loud enough to carry into the dressing room, "I need to eat something nourishing for a change. Can you hurry up? I'm getting light-headed."

"I think I found a swimsuit," she sang, then burst through the swinging doors. "What do you think?"

"Good Lord," the man muttered, his unlit cigarette bobbing.

Alan swayed, then gripped the side of the bench to steady himself. Pam's curves were stunning. Metallic gold, the top of the string bikini barely covered the tips of her generous breasts, the veed bottoms arrowed low to her bikini line and high on the sides, emphasizing the opposing curves of her waist and hips. His throat closed and perspiration popped out on his upper lip despite the chilling air conditioner.

Her pale eyebrows furrowed. "You don't like it."

"He loves it!" the man next to him shouted, his cigarette bouncing off the carpet. Then he punched Alan's arm so hard, Alan fell off the side of the bench.

Flat on his back, Alan wet his lips carefully, then croaked, "It will do."

6

"AREN'T YOU COLD?" Alan asked for the eleventh time.

Pamela jerked her head toward him, then lowered her ninety-nine-cent white sunglasses. "No."

"You look cold."

"Then stop looking." She leaned her head back against the plastic chaise lounge that suspended her several inches above the wet, white sand of the beach. "And stop talking."

After spending the day shopping with him yesterday and sharing an awkward dinner last night, she was ready to scream. They'd been at each other's throats all evening, culminating in an argument over finding someplace else to stay because he refused to sleep on the broken foldout bed. In the end, she had won separate sleeping arrangements, but he had complained about his back all morning.

Although quiet at the moment, he was driving her bananas, hiding behind those mirrored designer-prescription shades, reminding her every few seconds that she lay nearly naked within touching distance, yet he had no intention of doing so. Which was a good thing, she fumed, because she'd cuff his chiseled jaw if he laid a hand on her.

She harrumphed to herself. As if she would stoop to fooling around with her best friend's ex. Pam winced and concentrated, desperately trying to dissolve the sexual pull radiating from him.

After all, once they returned to Savannah, Alan might

run into Jo at an odd party or two, but Pam saw her at least a couple of times a week. Jo had been a true-blue friend, and Pam wasn't about to risk their relationship for a beach fling—no matter how pulse-poundingly gorgeous Alan looked lying glistening in the sun.

It was a glorious day, the sun as high as it could climb in a February Florida sky. As promised, the air temperature hovered in the mid-nineties, although she suspected the water temperature would be a bit more sobering. Still, it hadn't stopped several families from romping in the foamy waves, some with floats, some with masks to protect their eyes from the brine.

The beach was much more crowded than she'd expected. Portable stereos blared and the nutty smell of suntan lotion mingled with the salty air, barely masking the underlying scent of fish. Striped umbrellas populated the sloping stretch of pale sand and waitresses threaded their way through bodies to deliver drinks and hot dogs from the oceanside grill. The whole spring-break atmosphere was just another in a long series of surprises this trip had brought, she thought wryly, sneaking a sideways glance at Alan.

Bent over a book he'd bought at the mall, he looked relaxed and untroubled. Pam frowned sourly. *She* was wrestling with lewd and inappropriate thoughts, and *he* was reading a book.

"What is it now?" he asked, raising his head. "Is my breathing bothering you?"

Her gaze flicked across his oiled chest, watching defined bone and muscle expand and contract every few seconds, the sun dancing over every ripple. She could see her twin reflection in his gray lenses and wondered if he had any idea what he was doing to her. Unable to withstand the strain and confusion any longer, she swung her feet down, then stood, wrapping a short black sarong around her hips. "I'm going to stretch my legs."

Alan closed his book, keeping his place with one finger. "Want me to go along?"

Noting his uninterested tone, she shook her head. "I'll be back in an hour or so."

The strip of beach where fingers of water rolled in offered the clearest path for walking. She picked her way down to the front, ignoring a couple of low catcalls, then dug her toes in the cool, silky sand. Water hissed over her feet and frothed around her ankles, sending chills up her legs.

The beach snaked ahead of her, the people growing increasingly tiny in the distance, the shoreline curving left, then right again and disappearing about a mile away. Pam inhaled deeply, then set off at a brisk pace. Nothing cleared a person's head like the wind, water and sky.

As she made her way down to the water's edge, more than one good-looking man passed her, jogging or walking the other way, and more than one looked interested. A small smile curved her lips. One way to fight her ridiculous distraction with Alan was to find another man to distract her. A Robert Redford look-alike ran by her and grinned. Pam turned to watch him run away from her. A little on the short side, but he was definitely a looker. He had turned around and was running backward, scanning her figure up and down. After plowing into a group of teenagers, he saluted and went on his way.

"Don't tell me you're alone," a deep, accented voice said behind her.

Startled, Pam turned and looked up into the glinting eyes of a dark-eyed, dark-haired stranger. He looked to be of Latin American descent, his deep brown skin set off by gleaming gold jewelry at his throat, wrist and left earlobe.

He grinned, exposing amazingly white teeth. Pam shivered. Dark, dangerous, good-looking…just her type.

"Uh, yes," she said, then added, "at the moment." A girl had to be careful in strange surroundings.

The man extended his long-fingered hand. He wore a diamond-studded horseshoe ring on his middle finger. "Enrico." The "r" rolled off his tongue seductively.

Pam smiled and put her hand in his. "Pamela."

"Ah, Pamela. Do you live here or are you on vacation?"

"Vacation."

"Then surely you have just arrived—I could not have overlooked such a beauty."

Enrico massaged her fingers between his. "I flew in from Savannah yesterday."

"A southern belle. I thought I detected a slight, how do you say—*drawl?*"

"Yes," she said, then gently extracted her hand. "Where are you from?"

"Puerto Rico, originally, but I have lived in the United States for several years."

Pam nodded congenially. "In Fort Myers?"

"No, I am vacationing, same as you." He leaned toward her and lowered his voice to a husky whisper. "And I was becoming *very* bored."

Odd, she felt nothing but indifference as he looked into her eyes. Not a sizzle or a zing. Not even a stir. "Well, I'd like to finish my walk," she said pleasantly, stepping around him. "It was nice to meet you, Enrico."

His eyes devoured her. "Until next time, Pamela."

She gave him a shaky smile, then trotted away. Pumping her arms to elevate her heart rate, she kept her eyes averted from passersby and walked two miles, past rows of resorts that ranged in appearance from posh to worse-than-the-

Pleasure-Palisades. Finally, the crowds thinned and the sand became coarse and strewn with sea debris.

Pam waded into the waves up to her knees to cool off, watching a group of wet-suited windsurfers in the distance. It looked like fun—maybe she'd try it before they left. Sighing, she wondered if she'd be able to find enough entertainment to fill the hours between now and Saturday. Anything to keep her mind off Alan.

Anything but Enrico, that is—the guy gave her the willies. Turning to retrace her steps, she felt a surge of anticipation at seeing Alan again, then instant remorse. So much for clearing her head. She spotted him while she was still several hundred yards away—he was hard to miss since he stood at attention smiling down at a willowy brunette.

Absurd barbs of jealousy struck her low, but she squashed them. The woman was striking, thin and elegant in a simple black one-piece, wearing a large hat that shaded her face. The thought struck Pam that the woman might have been Jo's sister, she resembled her friend so closely. Regal, demure, classy...definitely Alan's type. Pam bit her lower lip, wondering if he wanted privacy, but knowing she needed sunscreen. Oh, well, she'd just swing by to pick up the lotion, then perhaps she could find the Robert Redford runner again.

Alan smiled and nodded to the lady, his book abandoned, Pam noted wryly. Above the music and the general din of the crowd, his voice floated to her in snatches as she approached the couple. "Show companies...become more productive...automation...accessibility."

The woman looked very impressed, nodding thoughtfully and lifting her expressive eyebrows. Her voice was lilting and definitely *interested.* "Client-servers...centralization...remote stored procedures."

Aha—a she-nerd. Out of all the people on this beach,

how had they found one another? Pam sighed. Just like Enrico, the tongue-rolling Romeo, had found her—birds of a feather, yada, yada, yada. Oh, well, if Alan was occupied, the temptation to jump his bones would definitely be removed…or at least reduced. "Hi," Pam said cheerfully as she approached the computer couple.

"Oh, hi," Alan said, smiling awkwardly.

"Don't mind me," Pam said, waving a hand. "I just came back to get sunscreen."

"Um, this is Robin," he said, gesturing to the woman, who pursed her lips at the sight of Pam.

"Hiya, Robin," Pam said, nodding to the woman. "Nice hat."

"Thanks," Robin replied slowly, then turned to Alan. "I guess I'll be going."

"Don't leave on my account," Pam assured her, holding up her lotion triumphantly.

"No, that's all right," the woman continued. "My friends will be wondering where I've gone." She smiled at Alan and swept his figure, head to toe. "I certainly hope we run into each other again."

Alan's tongue appeared to be tied, so Pam stepped in. "I'm sure you will—he'll be here until Saturday." She leaned toward the woman and lowered her voice conspiratorially. "He's available, you know."

The woman smiled awkwardly, then glanced from Pam to Alan.

"Pam—" Alan protested, but she waved her hand frantically to shut him up.

"And you are…?" the woman asked with a small laugh.

"Alan's sister," Pam said without missing a beat. "I'm Pamela." Alan made a small choking noise, but she ignored him.

"Oh." The woman nodded agreeably. "Well, it's nice

to meet you...Pamela." She winked. "And I'll see *you* later, Alan."

"Don't be a stranger," Pam sang as the woman walked away.

"What was that all about?" Alan demanded when she turned around. His arms were crossed over his broad chest, his pale eyebrows high over his shades.

Pam shrugged, her movements mirrored twice in his dark lenses. "It's plausible—we have the same coloring. Besides, who's going to believe the real story?"

Alan threw his hands up in the air. "I give up trying to follow your logic."

Falling into the chaise, Pam smeared sunscreen all over, down to the crevices between her peach-lacquered toes. Alan reclaimed his chair and his place in the book he was reading. She glanced at the cover and smiled. "Hey, *Dr. Moonshadow.* I thought it was the best book in the entire series."

He glanced over. "You've read the Light Years series?"

She nodded enthusiastically. "Have you gotten to the part where the Light Knights return with the king's head in a box?"

He dropped his head back on the chair, looking mortified. "That would be, I take it, *the ending?*"

Pam bit her lip. "Oh...yeah, I guess it would be."

Tossing the book in the sand a few feet away, Alan cursed and pushed himself to his feet. "Now *I'm* going for a walk."

Pam watched him stride off, admiring his defined hamstrings and calves. And she didn't miss the head-turning that spread through the women on the beach like "the wave" as he walked by. Oh, well, she decided as she fished in her purse for her cellular phone and a pad of paper, maybe he'd run into Robin the RAM/ROM woman.

Pam pulled out the phone's antenna, then stabbed in a number with the end of a pencil. Then maybe *she* could stop thinking about how much she enjoyed teasing Alan, how many interests they shared, how sexy— "Hello?" she responded to the voice on the end of the line, then realized her client, Marsha Wingate, had updated the message on her service.

"Hello, this is Madame Marsha, psychic in training, Monday, February twelfth. If this is Ronald, son, wear your guardian pendant today. I communed with the weatherman this morning through the television and the winds today in Syracuse are *definitely* unfriendly. If this is Sara, dear, don't talk to any Aries men today, and don't drink the tap water. If this is Lew, give me a trifecta twenty-dollar bet on the number three, four and seven greyhounds in the fifth race. And if this is Pamela, I drove by the Sheridan house last night precisely at midnight, and the bad vibes coming from that place—jeez, Louise! I want an expert's opinion, though, so I arranged to have a crystal reader from Atlanta drive down tomorrow. If this is anyone else, I have nothing to say, so don't bother to leave a message."

After the tone, which sounded vaguely like the theme from "The Twilight Zone," Pam left an upbeat message telling Mrs. Wingate she was out of town for a few days, but could be reached through her cellular phone if she decided to scoop up the Sheridan house before someone else got wise to what a steal it was. Smiling wryly at her own transparent sales tactic, Pam then checked into the office to let them know she didn't have her pager.

When she had exhausted every nit-picking phone call she could think of, she winced at the still-strong recharged battery light on her phone, then sighed and dug out the scrap of paper on which she'd written her friend Jo's new phone number. With her heart pounding guiltily, Pam punched in the numbers and prayed no one would answer.

"Heh-wo?" said a young voice.

"May I speak to Jo, please?"

"Jo-mommy?"

Pam blinked. Boy, did that sound weird—her friend Jo, a mommy. The littlest one must have picked up the phone, she decided. And although she was no expert on kids, he seemed way too young to be answering the phone. "Yes, Jo-mommy," she said carefully. "Go get Jo-mommy."

"Hello?" another voice said, this one slightly older. "Who is this?"

Pam frowned. "Who is this?"

"This is Peter Pa—I mean, this is Jamie Sterling. Who do you want?"

The middle one, she decided. "I need to speak with Jo."

"What for?"

Taking a deep breath, Pam forced a soothing lilt into her voice. "Just to talk—I'm a friend of hers." Then she heard the sound of the phone being ripped from his hand, followed by a scuffle and at least two raised kid voices as they tried to claim ownership of the phone, which was being bounced around the room.

"Hello?" A girl's voice came over the line. Jamie was still yelling something in the background.

The oldest one, Pam remembered. An owlish-looking little thing. "May I speak with Jo, please?"

"May I ask who's calling?"

At least she was polite. "This is her friend Pamela."

"She's indisposed at the moment."

Pam pulled back and looked at the phone. Indisposed? Quite a vocabulary for a tyke. "I'm calling long distance—are you sure she can't come to the phone?"

"She and my daddy are upstairs jumping on the bed."

With pursed lips, Pam nodded to herself. Of course. Where else would they be? Before she could think of an appropriate reply, Jo's voice came on the line. "Hello?" she asked breathlessly.

"Gee, Jo, can't you guys control yourselves at least until the kids go to bed?"

"Pam!" Jo laughed. "It's not what you think—John is testing the springs on the new mattress."

"Oh, is *that* what married folk call it?"

Jo laughed again, this time harder. She sounded almost giddy, Pam thought irritably, despite the clatter in the background. "Oh, never mind, Pam. I called your office this morning and they said you were out of town. Let me guess—Nick the All-Nighter?"

Pam squirmed on the lounge chair. "No."

"Delectable Dale?"

Sweat beaded on her upper lip. "Uh, no."

"Someone new?"

After mustering her courage, Pam muttered, "I'm with Alan in Fort Myers."

"Excuse me? Hang on a minute." Jo put down the phone, then Pam heard the sound of a police whistle peal shrilly, followed by, "QUI-I-I-I-I-ET!" The clatter ceased, then Jo picked up the phone. "Sorry. Now, what did you say?"

Pam tried again. "I'm with Alan in Fort Myers."

"You're with Alan in Fort Myers?" Jo asked, her voice richly colored with surprise.

"Yes, I'm with Alan in Fort Myers." It was getting easier to say, but she still felt as if she was going to have a stroke. She took another deep breath. "He decided to take the trip anyway. I gave him a ride to the airport, and he talked me into coming along. I haven't had a vacation in over a year, and he was acting a little desperate—"

"Pam," Jo cut off her rambling. "You are the best friend a woman could ask for."

Swallowing guiltily, Pam ventured, "I—I am?"

"I've been so worried about Alan. Now I can relax because I know you're looking out for him. How is he?"

Pam paused, thinking of all the just plain looking *at him* she'd been doing since they arrived. "He's a little depressed, which is normal, I guess."

"I'm sure his ego is bruised," Jo said mournfully. "I feel terrible. Can you try to cheer him up?" she pleaded. "Maybe take him dancing or do something fun?"

Pam's hands were so sweaty she nearly dropped the phone. Manufacturing a little laugh, she said, "Well, I'm not so sure the words *Alan* and *fun* can coexist, Jo, but I'll give it a shot."

"Make him extend himself a little," Jo urged. "Maybe he'll meet his soul mate while he's there—or at least have a little beach fling."

"He's certainly getting a lot of female attention," Pam agreed, failing to mention how much of it had derived from her.

"Good. Eventually Alan will realize we weren't right for each other, and that our marriage would never have worked. But for now, he could probably use a diversion."

"Right," Pam said as if she were receiving an assignment. "So, how's married life?"

"Wonderful," Jo said. On cue, a hellacious howl erupted in the background. "Oops, gotta run. Thanks again, Pam—you're a savior. Bye!"

Pam frowned at the silent phone. Savior? Sinner, perhaps, with all the wicked thoughts about Alan spinning in her head. She bit her lower lip—she should have gone to mass yesterday morning.

"What's wrong?" Alan asked as he dropped into his

lounge chair, his body gleaming with perspiration. He picked up a towel and wiped his face. "Did the FDA issue a moratorium on fried foods?"

She smirked. "No. I talked to Jo."

He stilled, then pressed his lips into a straight line. "You mean, Jo *Sterling?*"

"Um, yeah."

Alan lay his head back and Pam's heart twisted at the hurt on his face. "And how are the newlyweds?"

"Busy, from the noise in the background."

"Did you tell her where we are?"

Pam studied her nails. "Yeah. She seemed relieved."

He made an indignant sound. "You mean that I haven't self-destructed?"

"Well, she didn't use those words."

"She wouldn't have."

"I think she really does feel bad about what happened, Alan."

A deep sigh escaped him. "I'd rather not talk about it."

"Fine," Pam said, also eager to drop the subject. She glanced toward the water, then noticed a young man had set up shop on the beach, guarding a half-dozen Wave Runners bobbing in shallow water.

He picked up a megaphone and yelled, "Rent a Wave Runner, by the hour, by the half hour."

"Let's do it," Pam said, clambering out of her chair.

"Do what?"

"Rent a Wave Runner," she said, tugging on his hand.

"They look dangerous," Alan said with a frown.

"Can you swim?"

"Yes," he answered indignantly.

"Then come on, take a risk for once in your life."

He pushed himself up slowly, then followed her at a

leisurely pace. "I'm a risk-taker," he defended himself tartly.

"Oh, sure, Alan," she said over her shoulder. "You're a regular daredevil."

Alan bit his tongue. She was the most infuriating woman! He wanted to shake her, but he suspected that putting his hands on her and giving her breasts an excuse to jiggle would probably undo him in his current state. She strutted away from him, giving movement to the rub-on flower tattoo he'd watched her apply to her hip this morning in the room—a performance he'd been able to endure only by virtue of much teeth-grinding. His jaws still ached.

The young rental man was so bedazzled by Pam and her little bikini, he could scarcely speak. Amidst the boy's nods and a dancing Adam's apple, Alan halfheartedly negotiated a price for a Wave Runner and two wet suits, still unconvinced he would relish the ride.

Pam poured herself into a full-length neon pink wet suit with a built-in life jacket whose front zipper simply could not accommodate her chest. But leaving the zipper down a few inches only lifted her breasts higher and further emphasized her deep cleavage. Alan pulled on his own rubber suit, which was about six inches too short in the arms and legs. He performed a deep knee bend to loosen the material.

"I'll drive," Pamela announced, grabbing the handlebars and floating the Wave Runner out a few feet into the shallows.

"Oh my God," Alan gasped when he waded into the bracing cold water. "Are you sure this is going to be enjoyable?"

She scrambled up on the bobbing machine, straddling the bright yellow vinyl seat and plugging in the ignition starter. After slipping the stretchy key ring over her wrist, she turned around and held out her hand. "Would you stop complaining and get on?"

"What's that for?" he asked, pointing to the wristband that connected her to the machine.

"It's like a kill switch," she said with a grin. "If I throw us off, the engine dies."

"Oh, that's comforting," he said as he gingerly climbed up on the back and settled behind her on the long padded seat.

She pushed a button and the engine purred to life. "Better hang on," she warned over her shoulder as she turned the handlebars quickly and revved the engine, sending them into a sideways spin.

Alan grabbed the strap across the seat and managed to hang on, barely. "Have you ever done this before?" he shouted into the wind.

"Too many times to count," she yelled, leaning low and feeding the gas until they were hurtling across the waves at a breathtaking speed. They caught a wave, rode off the edge into the air, then landed with a teeth-jarring—and frigid—splash. Pam squealed in delight, then shouted, "You're throwing us off balance. Hang on to me!"

Too shaken and waterlogged to refuse, he wrapped his arms around her waist, twining his fingers into the buckles of her wet suit. She was going to kill him. Was drowning a painful way to die? In this case, he'd probably have a heart attack first. The air whooshed from his lungs as they landed hard and a wave of freezing water swelled over the back and drenched him. At this rate, he might suffer both tragedies in the space of the next few seconds.

Several hundred feet offshore, they zigzagged the water many times, and Alan could feel her confidence growing with each pass. He could have simply let go to escape the frenzied ride, but he had to admit the experience was rather thrilling. He jammed his body up behind hers, holding fast to her waist and pressing his face into her wet hair, giving in to the sexual zing that pierced his abdomen at holding her so close and bumping against her with every jump and spin.

She drove faster and faster, jumping higher and higher, landing with belly-flipping spinouts. When they caught the underside of a particularly deep wave, Alan sensed impending doom. Pam screamed in delight, and they were airborne for what seemed like a minute, when Alan decided they would be safer to land separate from the Wave Runner. He lifted his arms to clasp her, harness-style, then twisted off to the side, taking her with him, but releasing her before they hit the water.

He plunged in, bubbles fizzing around his ears, his senses temporarily clogged with the glug, glug of enveloping water. With two powerful kicks, he reached the surface, then slung water from his eyes and immediately looked for Pam.

Alan spun all around, treading water, frantically searching for a flash of neon pink, but he saw nothing except the silent wave runner several yards away and endless foamy green-gray waves.

7

ALAN'S HEART SLAMMED against the wall of his chest and panic coursed through his veins. "Pam!" he shouted, "Pam, where are you?" He swam toward the Wave Runner using long strokes, swallowing great gulps of cold, salty water as waves pushed and pulled at him, elevating his terror. She could have hit her head on the machine when he pulled her off...she could have hit the water at an odd angle and broken her silly neck...she could have been dragged down by an undertow...she could have—

"Of all the...stupid...things...to do!"

Alan stopped, then went weak with relief as he realized her voice came from the other side of the Wave Runner. She coughed fitfully until she gagged, then coughed more, wheezing, cursing him with every breath. He swam around to find her clinging to the side of the water bike, her golden hair molded to her head and neck, her mouth open to take in as much air as possible. She confronted him with wide, blazing blue eyes.

"Were you trying to kill me?" she croaked, then another coughing spasm overtook her.

"*Me?*" Alan yelled. "I was trying to keep you from killing us *both!* We would have been thrown off for sure on that last kamikaze maneuver!"

"Would not!"

"Would too!"

"Would *not!*"

"Would *too!*"

Pam stuck her tongue out at him, then reached up to climb back on the Wave Runner. "Next time I'll leave you on the beach with your book."

Alan shook with fury. First she'd given him the scare of his life when he thought she'd drowned, then she yelled at him for spoiling her fun! "Wait just a minute," he said, grasping her arm and pulling her back into the water.

"Let go of me!"

"I'm driving back."

"Oh no you're not!"

He squeezed her upper arm and pulled her face near his. "Oh yes," he said with finality, "I am."

Her eyes widened slightly in surprise, then her mouth tightened, but she didn't argue. A drop of water slid off the end of her nose and Alan once again marveled at the smoothness of her skin. The thought crossed his mind that she was close enough to kiss, but he was pretty sure she'd drown him if he tried. Her chest heaved with her still-labored breathing, straining the already taxed wet-suit zipper to near bursting. His body leaped in painful response because there was nowhere in his wet suit to expand. But the flash of pain brought him back to reality and he released her slowly, then moved away to a safer distance.

His brain had been scrambled from Pamela's joyride, Alan reasoned as he pulled himself out of the water to straddle the Wave Runner. He took a deep, head-clearing breath before turning around to offer his hand to help Pamela climb up. Her mouth quirked left, then right, but finally she let him help her up. She slipped a couple of times, which made him laugh, then she went limp with giggles and sank back into the water.

"You," he said, shaking his head, "are wearing me out."

"Then you," she said, heaving herself up far enough for him to pull her onto the seat, "don't have much endurance." She handed him the wristband.

"I never needed it with Jo," he said as she slid behind him. He bit the inside of his cheek and turned over the engine, immediately regretting mentioning his ex.

But Pamela simply reached around his waist and laced her hands together, then said close to his ear, "But I'm not Jo, am I, Alan?"

Her breath felt warm against his cold, wet ear, and her words swirled round in his head, taunting him. *I'm not Jo, am I, Alan?* An understatement of gigantic proportions. *I'm not Jo, am I, Alan?* As if he weren't electrically aware of the fact. *I'm not Jo, am I, Alan?* And he realized with a jolt that he was having fun, more fun than he'd had in a long time—and he was very glad that Pam was, well…just Pam.

His heart strangely buoyed, he tossed a mischievous smile over his shoulder and said, "Hang on." Then he leaned low over the handlebars and mashed the gas with his thumb, sending them lunging forward. Pam squealed in surprise and delight, ramming herself up against him, which tempted Alan to squeal with delight. He mimicked her earlier technique, driving fast, catching waves and landing with a spin, drenching them with walls of water that surged over the back. Adrenaline pumped through him and, combined with the sheer physical thrill of being close to Pamela, for the first time in his life he felt blatantly cocky.

Alan threw back his head and whooped, reveling in the pressure of Pam's thighs squeezing his. For several minutes, he sent them skimming and jumping over the sun-drenched water, slowing at last as their time remaining slipped to less than ten minutes.

Hating to see the ride end, he adjusted the speed to idle

and guided them toward the rental stand several hundred yards away. All sorts of strange and inappropriate emotions were running rampant through his body, and they were all directed toward Pam, who hadn't relaxed her hold around his waist. Waves slapped against the sides of the Wave Runner, and the sounds of beach music rolled out to meet them. Although sunset was still hours away, the beach was emptying rapidly as the locals packed up their families to go home for the evening meal.

"Did you have fun?" she asked, resting her chin on his left shoulder.

For a split second, Alan considered lying—he had an uneasy feeling that admitting he enjoyed Pam's company was not in his immediate best interests. But for the past hour, he had laughed more than he would have thought possible only a few hours ago, and for that, he owed her the truth. "Yeah, I did have fun. Thanks for taking my mind off...you know."

"What are friends for?" Pam asked lightly, closing her eyes and swallowing her guilt. She'd promised Jo she'd make sure he had fun. But at some point during their outing, she had forgotten she was supposed to be entertaining Alan because she was having such a good time herself. And now, putting back toward shore, she felt deflated and angry with herself for even thinking there wouldn't be too many excuses this week to hold Alan so close.

"Maybe we can take it out again tomorrow," Alan suggested, turning his head and inadvertently bringing his smooth cheek next to her mouth.

"Sure," she said casually, already looking forward to the ride. "Unless you'd rather take Robin."

"Who?" he asked, his tone innocent.

"My, what a short memory we have," she noted dryly. "You know, the smart woman in the hat."

"What makes you say she's smart?"

"Well, she works with computers, doesn't she?"

"The computer industry has its share of incompetents."

Pam brightened. "So she isn't smart?"

"Oh no, she's smart," he corrected, evoking a little stab of jealousy in her. "But don't assume anything just because someone talks in acronyms."

"You're getting sunburned," she said irritably.

He laughed and they pulled up next to the rental stand. "Are you sure it isn't the reflection from your suit?"

The young rental man had walked out into the shallows to meet them. Pam reluctantly relinquished her hold on Alan and dropped into the water up to her knees, already tugging at the confining zipper. By the time she reached the warm sand, she'd only managed to peel the rubber suit from one shoulder and she was already exhausted. She fell to the sand, knowing the grit would only make things worse, but she didn't care.

Lying on her back, she squinted against the sun and watched Alan extricate his magnificent body from his too-small suit with great sucking sounds as the rubber relented. Her breasts tightened in awareness and desire struck her low as he dragged the suit down, yanking his conservative navy trunks low on his hips. Standing in the sun with gleaming wet skin, his fair hair dry and tousled, he looked healthy and sexy, and Pam acknowledged for the first time that she was very attracted to him. And in more than just a physical sense, although simply looking at him had become a favorite pastime.

Today when he'd driven the Wave Runner, she had seen a side of him she'd never glimpsed before: carefree and spontaneous. He was actually fun to be with.

"Need a hand with your suit?" he asked, standing over her and grinning.

Pam nodded and took the hand he offered her, allowing herself to be pulled to her feet. She tugged at the opposite shoulder of the suit and succeeded in budging it an inch or so. Alan reached for the collar. "It's harder now that your skin is wet and the suit is heavy."

His fingers felt like branding irons against the cold flesh of her collarbone. He gripped the thick material and peeled the suit down her arm, turning the sleeve inside out. With both arms free, Pam was able to work the suit past her hips with some self-conscious wriggling, but had to admit defeat at her thighs. Then she lost her balance and sat down hard in the sand. Alan howled with laughter, but before she could get her breath to chew him out, she was thrown to her back because he had yanked her legs in the air to finish stripping off the stubborn suit. Sprawled in the awkward position and at his mercy, Pam felt like a too-big toddler being changed, and bristled at the hoots and laughter of the sparse but rapt audience staked out under umbrellas in the sand around them.

Alan also appeared to be enjoying her discomfort. At last he held up the pink garment as if it were a trophy and said, "I don't think this suit will ever be the same," then gestured to the deformed top of the fatigued-looking rubber suit. The comment brought him cheers from the members of the male gallery within earshot.

Pam scrambled to her feet, not sure if she liked this new, cocky side of Alan. "Well, while you strut for the other roosters," she said with a deceptively sweet smile as she brushed the sand from her bottom, "I'm going to find a beer."

Then she turned to march back to their blanket and chaise lounges they had rented for the day.

"Better go after her," some guy yelled to Alan behind her back.

"I'll go," another male voice piped up, triggering more laugher. But Pam had to acknowledge a little thrill that everyone assumed she and Alan were together.

"Hey," Alan said, jogging up beside her with a sheepish grin. "I'm thirsty, too."

Pam glanced at him, increasingly alarmed at the pull she felt toward him. "You need sunscreen."

He scrunched up his face and rubbed his cheek. "My skin does feel a little tight."

"Uh-oh," she warned. "Wait until after sundown."

He stepped in front of her, stopping her in her tracks. With eyebrows raised, he asked, "What will happen after sundown?"

Pam's pulse skipped and, not without a certain amount of panic, realized Alan was also feeling the sexual pull between them. His eyes searched her face, and she sensed that, ever the gentleman, he was waiting for a signal. They had reached the sticky point where everything they said to each other could be stretched, warped and misshapen to mean something else, an unstable area that might lead them to ruin unless one of them took control. And since Alan was freshly wounded from Jo's rejection, he was vulnerable to sexual revenge, even if he wasn't conscious of his motivation. And it was Pam's job to make sure that she wasn't a physical party to his retaliation for being dumped at the altar.

She forced lightness into her tone, ignoring his invitation to prolong the flirtation. "Sunburns are always worse after sundown," she said quietly, glad they had reached their chairs. She tossed him a bottle of sunscreen and pulled a short mesh cover-up over her head. Pointing up the sandy incline, she said, "I'm going to get a beer."

"Sounds great," he said, grabbing a T-shirt, but Pam held up her hand.

"Stay here and I'll bring them back," she said, desperate to escape his proximity. She practically ran up the stone path to the grill, but told herself she'd have to find a way to steel herself against the magnetism that had materialized between them—they would be here another four days!

The grill turned out to be a charming little outside eatery comprising a long bar and three weathered multilevel decks covered with latticed-wood "ceilings" that allowed the sun and wind to filter through. Pam glanced over the crowded tables, then walked to the bar and ordered two draft beers.

"Ah, Pamela, we meet again," came a deep, rolling voice behind her. Pam turned to see the handsome Enrico standing with an umbrellaed drink in his bejeweled hand.

"Er, yes," Pam said, offering him a small smile. As dangerous as the man appeared, at the moment he seemed the safer of two choices.

"Have you been enjoying the afternoon?" he asked conversationally, straddling a stool next to where she stood. His chest was well-developed and covered with dense, black hair. Pam made a split-second comparison to Alan's sleek physique, then bit the inside of her cheek when she acknowledged her preference.

"Sure," she answered casually, as the bartender slid two beers toward her.

"A two-fisted drinker?" he asked, his dark eyes dancing.

"For a friend," she explained, lifting one of the cups to her mouth with a shaky hand. Her revelations about Alan had her completely rattled.

"A male friend?"

Pam nodded.

Enrico formed a pout with his curvy mouth. "Is he jealous?"

Pam pressed her lips together, stalling. "I don't know," she said, licking the bittersweet liquid from her lips.

He made a clicking sound with his cheek. "Silly man." Then he leaned forward and wrapped a long blond lock around his forefinger. "I would never let you out of my si—iiiiIIIIEEE!" Enrico jerked back as a large arm descended between them on the bar with a resounding smack.

Pam swung her head up and gasped to see Alan standing between them, nursing a smirk. "I was getting thirsty," he said.

Anger flashed through her. How dare he show up while she was trying to forget about him! "Alan," she protested, "what are you doing?"

He nodded at the dark man he towered over. "Is this guy bothering you?"

"No!" she snapped.

"Excuse me," Enrico said, pushing away from the bar slowly. "Perhaps I'll see you later," he said, lifting his bronzed hand in a wave. Then he walked away, sipping his drink.

Alan watched him, then muttered, "Someone should tell him his back needs a trim."

"What the heck was that all about?" Pam demanded.

"I was defending your honor," Alan declared hotly. "*Again.* And a lot of thanks I get—again."

"Well, I guess I'm finally getting a glimpse of the real you, Alan P. Parish," she said through clenched teeth. "Tell me, does the 'P' stand for 'prehistoric'?"

He glared.

"Or 'paternal'?"

He glared.

"Or just plain 'putz'?"

He straightened and picked up his beer. "I can take a hint—if you want that...that gorilla with all his gold chains, then who am I to stand in your way. But if you start choking on a hairball, don't come crying to me."

A shrill ringing stopped him. Pamela reached inside her purse and pulled out her cell phone, then flipped down the mouthpiece. "Hello?"

"Pam?" Jo asked.

"Oh, hi, Jo," she said for Alan's benefit.

He frowned and took a huge gulp of beer.

"I was hoping I could talk to Alan," Jo said. "You know, explain what happened."

"Alan?" Pam asked, raising her eyebrows.

He shook his head no and waved his arms frantically, mouthing the words "No way."

"Uh, you just missed him," Pam said. "He went to get a beer."

"Are you both having fun?" Jo asked.

"Oh, yeah," Pam said, laughing merrily. "Fun, fun, fun."

"Oh, good," her friend answered. "Would you tell Alan I called and that I hope we can talk when he gets back?" She hesitated. "And that I'm really sorry for how things turned out?"

"Sure thing," Pam said, giving Alan a tight smile.

"And Pam," Jo said. "Thanks again for being such a good friend to me and to Alan."

"Don't mention it," Pam answered, then folded up the phone. "Jo said she hopes the two of you can talk when you get back, and that she's really sorry for how things turned out."

Alan downed the rest of his beer, then slid the plastic cup across the bar for a refill. "On second thought, I think I'll stay right here and get drunk," Alan said, settling on the stool Enrico had vacated.

Pam rested one hip on the corner of the neighboring stool. "I don't know if that's such a good idea," she warned with a half smile. "The last time you got drunk, you invited me to go on your honeymoon."

One corner of his mouth lifted. "This is one for the record books," he said, shaking his head. "Do you suppose I'm the only man in history who won't get laid on his honeymoon?"

"Well," Pam said slowly, "it doesn't have to be that way." When his eyes widened, she stammered, "I m-mean, there are lots of women on the b-beach..." Flustered, she swept her hand in the air. "Take what's-her-name in the hat."

"Robin," he said, then began draining his second beer.

"Robin!" she seconded, nodding. "Nice teeth."

"Cute figure," he said.

"If you go for the boyish look," Pam agreed, still nodding.

"Nice legs," he said.

"Thick ankles," she murmured.

"Pretty hair."

"Sloppy dye job."

"Are we talking about the same woman?" Alan asked, angling his head. "I talked to her for twenty minutes and you saw her for what—twenty seconds? How did you notice all those things?"

Pam shrugged. "A woman knows."

"I thought she was nice."

"She was nice," Pam agreed. "*If* you're going to settle for nice."

"What's wrong with nice?" Alan asked.

"It's boring."

"One person's boredom is another person's reliability."

She sighed, exasperated. "We're talking about a beach fling, Alan. Reliability doesn't even make the list." She turned and gestured to the crowd around them, deciding she'd have to get the ball rolling for him. "Look—women everywhere—just pick one."

Alan turned slowly on the stool. "You make it sound so, so…"

"Spontaneous?"

"I was going to say cheap."

"What about the redhead in the corner?" she asked, pointing her pinkie.

"She's cute," Alan agreed with a halfhearted shrug.

"Well, don't get too excited," she warned sarcastically. "I suppose you prefer brunettes."

"Not really," he said, draining his beer and smiling. "It's been a while since I went looking for a woman, but I don't think I discriminate."

Pam finished her beer and accepted a refill. She was already getting a buzz since she hadn't eaten much all day. "How about the one in the green bikini?"

He looked and squinted. "She's kind of skinny, don't you think?"

"I thought men liked skinny women."

"Slender, great. Curvy, even better. But skinny, no way," he said, shaking his head.

"The yellow shorts and piled-up hair?"

"A definite possibility," he conceded slowly.

Pam frowned and gulped her beer. "She laughs like a seal, though. I can hear her barking from here."

"Wow, look at the one in the red suit," he said, leaning forward slightly.

Pam squinted, then dismissed her with a wave. "They're fake," she said with confidence.

"How do you know?"

"Can't you tell? They don't move."

"Well, she isn't on a trampoline. Besides—" he turned

a wolfish grin her way "—I hate to break it to you, Pam, but most men don't care if they're real or not."

"You don't have to tell *me* about men," she said.

He adopted an expression of mock remorse. "Sorry—I forgot I was talking to the source." He frowned. "I'm curious—is there a straight man in Savannah who isn't after you?"

She grinned. "Two Baptist reverends, and you."

Alan saluted her with his drink. "Gee, thanks—you do wonders for my ego. Ever been married?"

"Nope."

"How have you managed that?"

Pam ran a finger around the rim of the plastic cup and pursed her lips. Then she gave a little shrug and said, "I've never fallen in love."

He scoffed. "I think falling in love is a vicious rumor that was started thousands of years ago by the world's first wedding director."

She giggled, then sighed as memories washed over her. "I came close once—I was seventeen and looking for a way out of the projects. He was nineteen and had the world by the tail."

"What happened?"

"He also had two other girls by the tail."

"Oh."

"That's when I decided it was much safer to play the field rather than risking it all on one horse. And I've been hedging my bets ever since."

"Hey," he said, holding up his hand. "Forget the horses—I don't want to hear about the kinky stuff."

Pam giggled.

Alan polished off another beer. "What's your secret for staying single?"

"It's easy," she said. Leaning forward, she whispered, "Don't close your eyes."

"What?"

"When you kiss—don't close your eyes."

He looked dubious. "That's your secret weapon?"

She nodded emphatically, and noticed the room still bounced slightly even when she stopped. "When you close your eyes during a kiss, your mind starts playing all kinds of games. You start to imagine a make-believe world where love conquers all. And you forget that most marriages end in divorce—or worse."

"My parents seem pretty happy," he said.

"That's nice," she said, and meant it. "My dad split when we were little, so I barely remember my folks together."

"I'm sorry."

She smiled sadly. "Me, too. That's why I'd rather stay single and childless than risk dragging kids through a mess."

"I'm for the childless part," Alan noted wryly. "A toast," he said, lifting his cup to hers, "to keeping your eyes open."

"Hear, hear," she agreed, touching her cup to his, then giggled when beer sloshed over the side. A gust of cold air blew over them and Pam shivered. Dusk was approaching, and the temperature had dropped dramatically. "I think I'll go back to the room and change."

Alan climbed down from the stool slowly. "I need to check in with my secretary and see if she found us a room. I'm not anxious to spend another night in Hotel Hell."

"It's not so bad," she said as they walked, picking their way carefully back down the unlit path. The clear night and bright moon made the going easier, and the now-deserted white beach stretched below them like a wide satin ribbon.

"Ooh, look at all the stars," she said, waving her hand overhead. "Let's go for a walk."

"Anything to avoid going back to the room," he agreed, falling in step behind her.

She pulled loose pants from her canvas bag and stepped into them, then decided to carry her sandals. "The sand looks like snow," she said, digging in her toes. The tide was coming in, eating away at the beach and forcing them to choose a higher path. The air felt cool and invigorating and Pam tried hard to focus on anything but the romantic atmosphere as they headed down the beach toward their hotel. Millions of stars twinkled overhead and, as always, simply thinking about the distances their mere existence represented left her breathless. And coupled with the sight of Alan's handsome face silhouetted in the moonlight, she was left downright light-headed. "Alan, do you really think there's life on other planets?"

"Sure," he said without hesitation. "I think it's pretty arrogant to think the entire universe was created just for us."

She tingled in appreciation of his honesty—she could never broach this subject with any of the men she dated. "I agree—but it's a little scary, don't you think?"

He shook his head. "Nah, if they were going to harm us, they would have done it by now." Then he grinned. "Besides, with all our societal and environmental problems, Earth is probably the laughingstock of the universe."

"What you're telling me," she said with a chuckle, "is that I clawed my way out of one slum simply to exist in a larger one?"

"In a manner of speaking," he conceded with a laugh.

"Okay, the 'P' stands for 'pessimistic,' right?"

He laughed again, something she was beginning to look forward to. "So I'm not the most upbeat person, especially this week." He brushed against her accidentally and her arm burned from the contact. They walked past several tall dunes, which cast tall shadows over them, throwing them into almost complete darkness.

"What doesn't kill you will make you stronger," she said, wondering for whose benefit she was speaking—Alan's or hers? She stumbled on a clump of glass and yelped, grabbing Alan's arm on the way down. But she caught him off guard and he fell with her. Pam grunted when she landed, then was struck with the thought that being horizontal felt pretty good. She gingerly lifted her head and saw Alan sprawling face first next to her. When he raised onto his elbows, his face was covered with a layer of white sand. Pam burst out laughing.

"You," he said with mock fierceness, "are dead meat."

She shrieked and tried to scramble to her feet, but he grabbed her bare ankle and yanked her down to the sand. Weak with laughter, she tried to crawl away from him, but he dragged her back and rolled her over, pinning her arms down.

Her laughter petered out at the closeness of his face to hers in the darkness, and a warning siren screamed in her head. He lay half on top of her, his chest against hers. His T-shirt had worked up and she felt the warm skin of his stomach through the flimsy cover-up she wore. Every muscle in her body tensed and her pulse pounded in her ears. "Alan—" she said in a shaky voice.

"Pam," he cut in with a hoarse whisper, his breath fanning her lips. "Please don't tell me to stop, because then I'll have to."

She couldn't see his eyes, but she could hear the loneliness, the desperation in his voice. "Alan," she croaked with as much strength as she could muster.

He sighed slowly and lifted his head a few inches in resignation. "What?"

Seconds stretched into a minute as the waves crashed

behind them and the love scene in *From Here To Eternity* passed before her eyes. God, Alan was so sexy and so...so...so *here*. Who cared about eternity? "Kiss me," she said breathlessly.

For a while, he was completely still, and she wondered if perhaps he hadn't heard her. But then he lowered his mouth with such sweet slowness, she was able to anticipate the feel of his lips on hers and ready herself for his taste. His lips were like velvet, she thought, as her mouth opened for his. When his mouth met hers, Pam moaned at the surge of desire that swelled in her chest. If she had expected tentativeness, those expectations were banished immediately. It was as if his lips knew hers, as if they had explored the surface and depths of her mouth many times. His tongue boldly tangled with hers in a slashing, grinding dance and he shuddered, offering a deep groan that echoed down her throat.

The urgency of their kiss increased and he released her arms to seek out more forbidden areas. He caressed her collarbone, then blazed a trail south to cup her breast and thumb the beaded nipple, practically the only skin her bathing-suit top covered. She arched her body into him, and slid her hands under his shirt to feel the hard wall of muscle across his back. He kneed her legs open, then shifted to lie cradled between her thighs.

Longing pulsed through her body and moisture gathered at her core where he pressed the hard ridge of his erection against her. Slipping her hands below his waistband, she gripped the smooth rounds of his hard buttocks, her mind spinning with the responses he evoked from her body. He lifted his head and gasped, "Not here. Someone might—"

She cut him off with a deep kiss, then whispered, "The beach is deserted, no one will see us. Besides," she murmured, yanking his T-shirt over his head, "I think it's kind of exciting."

In a flurry of sand, she pushed down his trunks and dragged them off with her feet. He lay naked on top of her, kissing her deeply and kneading her covered breasts with a slow intensity that told her he planned to take his time undressing her, enjoying her. She writhed beneath him, urging him on with her wandering hands, anxious to explore his body.

Then a blinding light flashed over his shoulder, directly in Pam's eyes. "Hold it right there, mister," said a gruff male voice.

Alan stiffened, then lifted his head and swung to look over his shoulder. He raised his arm to shield his eyes. "What the hell?"

"Police," the man boomed, thumping his badge unnecessarily since the uniform said it all. "Stand up slowly and put your hands in the air."

Alan scoffed. "You can't be serious—"

"I said, on your feet!"

Pam's heart pounded in her chest and she squeezed her eyes shut, unable to watch. When she finally chanced a glance, Alan stood squinting into the cop's light with his arms in the air, hosting a monster erection.

"God," the cop said, wincing.

"I hope that means you'll let me find my pants," Alan snapped, outraged.

"Make it quick," the officer said. "I'd hate to haul you in naked."

"What?" Alan barked. Pam sprang up, her heart in her throat.

The cop gave him a sneering smile and pulled out a pair of handcuffs. "This is a family beach, you pervert. You're under arrest for indecent exposure."

8

"I'VE NEVER BEEN so humiliated in my life," Alan declared as he followed Pam out of the city jail and squinted into the late-afternoon sun. She looked chipper in her crisp white shorts and red silk blouse. He, on the other hand, still sported the sand-crusted swimming trunks and T-shirt he'd been wearing last night when the cop hauled him into jail like a common criminal. Between the cot he'd slept on and the realization that he and Pamela Kaminski had been minutes away from sharing carnal knowledge, he hadn't slept a wink.

"No one will find out," Pam said in a soothing voice.

"Oh, really?" he asked. "Is that like, 'It's deserted, no one will see us'?"

She frowned. "I said I was sorry a hundred times—didn't you hear me?"

"One hundred thirty-six times," he corrected. "I heard you during the entire walk to the squad car last night, *and* as you ran alongside the police car when we drove away, *and* this morning in the courtroom while the judge was lecturing me—" He stopped and stared toward the street in disbelief, then pressed his palms against his temples. "Pam, are you nuts?"

"What?" She pushed the cheap sunglasses high on her forehead and unlocked the door to the powder blue limo.

"You left this pimpmobile parked in a fire zone in *front* of the jail for two hours?"

She shrugged her lovely shoulders. "I turned on the hazard lights."

"Oh, well," he said with as much sarcasm as he could muster. "I didn't realize you'd turned on the *hazard* lights." He summoned a dry laugh. "After all, everyone knows that hazard lights cancel out every broken law. Mow down a pedestrian? No problem, just turn on your hazards."

"Well, it's still here, isn't it?" she demanded hotly.

"Who the hell else would want it?" he cried, feeling on the verge of hysteria.

She pointed to the passenger side. "Just get in, will you?"

"Oh, no," he said, holding out his hand for the keys. "You are *not* driving."

"I drove here without any problems!"

"Oh, really?" Alan crossed his arms, then nodded toward the front fender. "And I suppose that telephone pole–size dent just appeared from nowhere?"

She bit her bottom lip, and handed over the keys in silence.

"Thank you," he said, then opened the driver-side door just as a police car pulled up behind the limo with its siren silent but flashing. When the young cop stepped out, he had already begun writing the ticket.

"Sir," he said in a pleasant voice. "Do you have any idea what the fine is for parking in a fire lane in front of a government building?" Alan closed his eyes and counted to ten.

A few minutes later, Pam studied the pink carbon copy the police officer had given him and whistled low. "A hundred and forty-five dollars?"

"Do me a favor," he said calmly, gripping the steering

wheel so hard his hands hurt. "Just sit over there and don't talk."

"Look, Alan, I know you're upset—"

"Upset?" he crowed. "Just because I'm now considered a sex offender? Why would that upset me?"

"It's not as bad as you make it sound."

"Before yesterday, I'd never even received a speeding ticket."

Pam lay her head back. "Do you realize you can rearrange the letters in your name to spell 'anal'?"

He scowled in her direction. "I'm not going to apologize for being a law-abiding citizen."

"Your secretary called last night."

His stomach twisted. "You talked to Linda?"

"Relax, I told her I worked for the hotel and all your calls were being routed to me. She found you a room."

"Finally, some good news," he said, his shoulders dropping in relief.

"I told her you changed your mind."

He weaved over the centerline. "What?"

"She needed an answer immediately, and I didn't know how long you'd be in jail…" Her voice trailed off and she raised her hands in a helpless gesture. Her manicured nails had gone from peach to bright red during his incarceration.

"I'll call her later to see if the room is still available," he said. "Right now, even the broken couch in Hotel Hell sounds good." Then the thought struck him that Pam might think they'd be sharing the same bed, after what nearly transpired last night. Except now that he'd had a few idle hours to ponder their lapse, he realized what a huge mistake it would have been. No matter how much he *wanted* to sleep with Pam, only a jerk would have rebound sex with his ex-fiancée's best friend. Besides, he admitted begrudgingly, as infuriating as she could be, Pam was starting to grow on him, and he didn't want to tread on their burgeoning friendship, didn't want to be relegated to her bottomless dating pool. "I'll call and see if the pullout bed can be fixed."

"Done," Pam said with a little smile. "This morning I slipped the maintenance man a twenty and he fixed it in no time."

"Great," Alan said, nodding.

"Yeah," she said.

After a pregnant pause, they both spoke at the same time.

"About last night—" she said.

"I want to apologize—" he said, then stopped and they both looked away and laughed awkwardly.

"It was the moon and the stars—"

"—and the beer and the ocean," she added.

"I was still feeling a little rejected over the wedding—"

"—and I was feeling lonely."

"What a big mistake it would have been," he said, attempting a casual laugh.

"Huge," she agreed.

"Gigantic—"

"Colossal—"

"What with you being Jo's best friend—"

"—and you being Jo's ex-fiancé."

Feeling relieved, Alan inhaled deeply. "So we're in agreement." Then he glanced over and realized with a sinking feeling that despite his new resolve, he still wasn't immune to her remarkable beauty.

"Completely in agreement," she assured him with a bright smile.

SHE HAD DONE a lot of stupid things in her relatively short life, Pam decided the next day as she lay in a rental chaise on the beach and watched a kidney-shaped cloud move across the otherwise clear sky. But all of them rolled into one wouldn't have compared to the absolute brainlessness she would have exhibited if that cop hadn't shown up the night before last.

Luckily, Alan seemed to agree with her and they had touched on, danced around and sidestepped the issue of their sexual attraction while somehow agreeing that the sex act itself would have been a grievous error. The logical side of her brain had no problem going along with that argument, but the emotional side of her brain kept remembering the feelings raging through her that night when Alan kissed her—after all her bragging, she had actually closed her eyes! And though she had definitely responded to him on a physical level, he had also stirred something deep inside her. Alan had accidentally managed to blaze a trail where no man had gone before, and the realization saddened her because a relationship between them was impossible. Unthinkable. Inconceivable.

He was still in love with her best friend, for God's sake. And she wasn't about to return to Savannah arm in arm with Alan and have Jo think they had been carrying on behind her back all these years. Besides, Alan P. Parish came from Savannah's most prosperous family, while she came from Savannah's most pros*ecuted* family. He wouldn't be interested in anything other than a sexual relationship with her. Typically, such a revelation wouldn't bother her, but she was starting to feel a weird sort of affection for the man, striking a memory chord from when she'd first known him in high school. Warning bells chimed in her head and some untapped part of her soul telegraphed increasingly urgent distress signals.

SUBJECT IS DANGEROUS STOP HEART IN JEOPARDY STOP PROCEED WITH CAUTION STOP

"Our paths keep crossing." Enrico's undulating voice

wafted above her. Pam opened her eyes to see him standing over her, surveying her new red two-piece suit with open admiration. He wore a straw hat and snug little bikini swim trunks that Europeans seemed fond of wearing. Pam pressed her lips together in amusement at the recollection of Alan's scoffing reference to the shiny, elastic garments as "nut-huggers."

"It must be destiny," the dark-skinned man continued with a charming grin.

"Or just a small beach," she offered, making no movement to encourage him to stay. She had enough on her mind, and she felt her patience dwindling.

"Could I interest you in dinner tonight?" he asked. "I know a restaurant where the lobster is fresh and the drinks are strong." He wagged his dark eyebrows and Pam wondered where he or any other man had gotten the idea that women found the gesture provocative.

"I already have dinner plans," she lied. "Thanks anyway."

Enrico's expression grew sultry as he dipped his head. "And do you also have plans for dessert?" he asked, his meaning clear in the husky timbre of his voice.

"I'm on a diet," she said, smiling tightly. "Thanks anyway." Then she retrieved a book from her canvas bag and opened it.

"That man in the bar yesterday, he is your boyfriend?" Enrico pressed.

Pam glanced up from the book, suddenly at the end of her fuse. "No," she said with quiet authority. "He's my husband."

"Oh?" He looked surprised, then pulled a sad face. "And he has left you alone yet again."

"I wore him out," she said evenly, then looked back to her book.

Enrico must have taken the hint because he moved away after a tongue-rolling farewell, but she felt his dark gaze linger over her and shivered.

The book was one that Alan had purchased, one she'd devoured years ago, but it was worth another read. Especially if it took her mind off Alan, who lay spread-eagle on the water bed where he'd slept since returning from jail yesterday afternoon. She had eaten dinner alone last night and crawled into the lumpy pullout bed where she'd lain awake for hours thinking about the man only a few feet away.

She sighed and immersed herself in a world of fantasy and science fiction, caught up in interstellar wars, life and romance in the next millennium.

In the early afternoon, she gave in to hunger pangs and walked up the path to the grill. After ordering a messy hot dog, she sat down at a table overlooking the beach to sort through the last few days' disturbing turn of events.

The crowds had thinned a bit since the locals had resumed their midweek work schedules, leaving behind vacationers and snowbirds who seemed to group almost exclusively by twos. With a start, she remembered that today was Valentine's Day, so no wonder everyone was paired off—lots of folks were probably here for their anniversary since February fourteenth seemed to be a popular date for weddings. The bartender confirmed her theory by announcing a couples' sand castle–building contest for the remainder of the afternoon, with the winning pair to receive a romantic dinner at a local seafood restaurant.

Her mind wandered to Alan and she hoped he was resting. As if on cue, he emerged from the trees that hid the pebbly path below their balcony. To her dismay, her pulse kicked up as she watched him move with natural athleticism down the slight incline and out onto the white sand.

A towel lay around his wide shoulders, and he carried a small gym bag, which she surmised was full of books. His head pivoted as he scanned the area. Was he looking for her? she wondered with a little smile. Then he waved to someone farther down the beach and Pam forgot to chew the food in her mouth as she spotted Robin the Computer Lady and her big floppy hat.

Swallowing painfully, she watched as Robin stopped and waited for Alan to walk to her, which he seemed eager to do, she noted wryly. Today Robin wore a high-necked tank suit of boring brown, but Pam conceded her legs were long and slim. From a distance, the woman's resemblance to Jo was uncanny. She held on to her hat with one hand as she tilted her head back to smile up at Alan. Pam stabbed her chili dog with enough force to snap the plastic fork.

And Alan seemed to have recovered from his ill mood, she noticed as he offered the woman a broad smile. Robin gestured in the direction from which she'd come and Alan nodded happily, seemingly anxious to follow her...where? To her blanket? Pam sank her teeth into her bottom lip. To lunch? She shredded the paper napkin in her lap. To her room? Pam felt something akin to gas pain in her stomach. At least if he had a fling with Robin, she reasoned, the sexual tension hanging between herself and Alan would be relieved. And maybe they'd be able to get through the rest of the week and arrive back in Savannah with all friendships intact.

The computer couple stopped after a few steps and Robin squirmed, pointing to her shoulder. Alan stopped, investigated and brushed away the offending object. *Oh, brother—the old "something's on me, will you get it off, you big strong he-man" trick.* Pam rolled her eyes. *Amateur.*

But Alan must have been convinced because he inched

closer to Robin as they strolled away. When Pam could no longer see them from her chair, she stood up. When they disappeared past tiptoe level, she walked to the corner of the deck. "Go for it, Alan," she muttered as she hung out over the edge with her back foot hooked around the railing to keep from falling. "I couldn't care less."

THE POOL AT THE RESORT where Robin was staying glimmered blue and white, interrupted only by a few adults who lounged in one corner, with firm grips around their drinks. Alan sat next to Robin, bored with shoptalk and hoping something conversational would pop into his head. Accepting her invitation to join her at the pool had seemed like a good idea an hour ago, but now he was feeling restless. For some maddening reason, Alan couldn't keep his mind off where and with whom Pam had found entertainment for the afternoon.

"What's wrong?" Robin asked cheerfully.

"Nothing," he assured her. She was very attractive, and had pulled her chair so close to his she'd pinched her fingers between the two arms. And if he had any doubts she was interested in him physically, they were banished when he felt her bare foot caress his leg from calf to ankle. Startled, he stiffened.

She flashed him a flirty smile. "Want to take a swim? The pool is heated."

"Sure," he said, pushing back from the table, suddenly wanting to escape. He followed her into the shallow end, then swam the length of the pool, not at all surprised when she surfaced near him at the other end. With the concrete wall at his back, he closed his eyes and raised his face to the sun.

"Great day," she said, allowing her body to graze his beneath the water.

"Mmm." He really should find Pamela and apologize for being so cross yesterday.

"I always stay in this resort when I'm in town," she continued.

"Nice," he murmured.

"My room has a fabulous view," Robin said near his ear, and several seconds passed before her meaning sank in. She rubbed her breast against his arm and his eyes popped open.

Her mouth curved provocatively. "Want to go up for a look?"

Alan glanced at her and realized with a sinking feeling that she reminded him of Jo—in more ways than one. Although Jo had never been as forward as Robin, he experienced the same mild stirring of sexual interest when he looked at the slim woman in her sensible brown bathing suit. All the time he had dated Jo, he'd hoped their relationship would become more sensual, but now he had to admit that their chemistry had never been quite right. And while he had loved Jo from the beginning, he had never been *in* love with her...had never craved her company so much that he experienced physical pain when he was away from her...had never been tempted to get naked with her on a dark beach.

"Alan?" Robin whispered, moving in for a kiss. Her mouth shifted against his pleasantly and Alan tried to conjure up some level of desire, especially in light of his new revelation. He absolutely couldn't be falling for Pam....

Robin's mouth became more insistent and Alan awkwardly pulled her against him, running his hands over her slight curves and waiting for his body to respond.

She lifted her head, breathing heavily. "How about that view?"

Alan's mind raced. *Do it, Parish. Get Pam out of your*

head and out of your system. "Um, sorry," he said, withdrawing and pushing himself up and out of the pool. "I promised Pam I'd...take her shopping."

Robin stared at him from the water. "You'd rather go shopping with your sister?"

"No," he said hurriedly, grabbing his towel and gym bag. "It's just that I promised...I'll see you later, Robin."

"Count on it," she said pointedly, as if next time he would not get away so easily.

Alan trotted off in relief, then slowed to a walk when he reached the beach. He made his way back up the shore, keeping on eye on the horizon for a Wave Runner rider in an overflowing neon pink wet suit and wrestling with the bombshell of the feelings he harbored for his ex-fiancée's best friend.

Along the way, he noticed several sand castles, some simple, some intricate, and realized a contest was under way. A few hundred yards later, he noticed a loose knot of men had gathered to watch a work in progress. But as he approached, he recognized the fake flower tattoo on the firm hip of Pamela Kaminski. She crawled on all fours and stretched to add yet another tower to the elaborate castle she had created. He smiled wryly at the realization that although her sand fortress was by far the most impressive he'd seen, *Pam's* turrets were gaining far more attention than her castle's.

Seemingly oblivious to the attention, her head was bent in concentration, although she kept brushing back a strand of golden hair that had escaped the high ponytail. The red bikini was a masterpiece, he acknowledged, marveling at the way she filled it to bursting yet managed to keep everything safely in place as she moved around. His body began to harden at the memory of her lying beneath him in the sand. But knowing that train of thought led to a dead end, he forced himself to squash the provocative vision. Uncomfortable with the thought of being a part of the ogling crowd, he stepped forward and announced, "There you are!" in a loud voice.

Pam glanced up and smiled, then sat back on her heels, offering a mouth-drying view of her cleavage. Her breasts were confined by two tiny triangles of cloth that had to be much stronger than they looked. "Hi," she said, and Alan could almost hear the groans of dismay as the men realized their up-close perusal had come to an end. One by one, they drifted away.

"Are you alone?" she asked, peering around him.

"Yeah," he said, suddenly wondering how he could have been so angry with her yesterday.

She turned her attention back to the sand castle. "Have you been in bed all this time?"

"Pretty much," he said, shrugging. "But I feel much better."

"That's nice," she said tightly, but she didn't look up.

She was probably still miffed at him for the way he'd behaved yesterday afternoon, he reasoned. "I'm sorry I was so grouchy when you came to pick me up," he said, not sure why he felt the need to get back into her good graces. "I did appreciate it."

"It's okay," she said in a tone that didn't sound okay. Then she glanced over her shoulder. "You got it all out of your system, right?"

"Right," he said, hoping he looked properly contrite. "Truce?"

"Truce," she said with a suddenly cheerful smile, then stood and dusted sand from her knees.

"Hey," he said, studying her design. "You need a moat." He took one of the buckets she'd been using as a mold and filled it with water, then fed the small channel she'd dug around the perimeter of the castle. After several trips, the moat was filled, and she nodded, satisfied with his contribution.

"That's quite a spread, little lady," the bartender from the grill said as he made his way toward them. "Nice castle, too," he muttered to Alan with an envious wink as he walked by. The chubby fellow shook her hand and gave her an envelope. "The best sand castle by far—you two have a real nice Valentine's Day dinner." Then his expression turned serious. "Be careful after dark, though—I hear we have a pervert on the loose, some naked guy scaring women and little kids."

Alan frowned, but at least Pam managed to restrain herself until the man had walked away. "Pervert?" She threw her head back and laughed. "Is that what the 'P' stands for?"

"Ha, ha, very funny."

"Here," she said, handing him the envelope and wiping her eyes. "You and Robin have a nice evening."

"Robin?" He shook his head. "I've spent all the time with her today that I want to. What about Enrico?"

"Somehow I don't think he'd be much of a dinner companion," she said, and Alan got her meaning loud and clear: the man was a lover, not a talker. He tried to stem the jealousy that flooded his chest, but the thought of Pam with another man was crushing. Had she rendezvoused with the hairy horndog last night or this morning—or both?

"Looks like we're stuck with each other, then," he said with a casual shrug that belied the emotions raging through him.

"Looks like it," she said, falling a little short of looking happy at the prospect herself.

PIER TWENTY-EIGHT was bustling with couples celebrating Valentine's Day. Boasting a large bar, a roving Italian quartet and a great oceanside view, Pam could see why. As they waited at the bar for their table, she noticed Alan's gaze lingering on her again. Although she had hoped his little diversion with Robin would ease the situation, she had felt more on edge than ever while they were getting ready for dinner.

Just to be safe, she had emerged from the bathroom already dressed in a simple deep pink sleeveless sheath, but she'd felt him watching her while she piled her hair on her head with various combs. And she had to admit she struggled to keep her attention elsewhere while he applied lotion to his reddish shoulders before donning a dress shirt.

He did look fabulous, she decided, and allowed herself a bit of pride to be on his arm tonight. When they had attended functions together in Savannah, it had been different—everyone knew he was devoted to Jo, so Pam had never entertained thoughts of what kind of couple she and Alan might make. But now she knew they were garnering a fair share of attention, and she conceded they looked like a classic "match": tall with blond hair and glowing tans. But looks could be deceiving, she noted with a little twist of her heart.

"Well, if it isn't the newlyweds," a man's voice said behind her. Pam registered Alan's slight frown before she turned to see Cheek and Lila, the senior-citizen couple who, thankfully, they hadn't seen naked in a while.

"Cheek," Lila said with a motherly smile. "They're not married, remember? They're just friends, right?"

"Right," Alan and Pam said in unison.

"Wasn't it a lovely day?" Lila continued, waving vaguely toward the beach.

"Great dress," Cheek said bluntly, talking to Pam's breasts.

"Er, thanks," Pam said as Alan cleared his throat.

"You're getting a nice tan," Lila commented.

"I was on the beach all day," Pam told her.

"This beach?" Cheek asked in amazement. He leaned forward then glanced around as if he were about to divulge military secrets. "There's a nude beach about twenty miles away," he said in a conspiratorial tone. "It's five bucks a head, but it's worth it," he finished with an emphatic curt nod.

"We'll keep that in mind," Alan said tightly.

The man turned to Pam and said, "If you decide to go, we'd be glad to give you a ride."

"I said," Alan said, his tone louder and his expression harder, "we'll keep it in mind."

"Great," Cheek said, completely missing the rebuff. "You want to see if we can get a table for four?"

"No!" Pam and Alan nearly shouted together.

"Uh, it's a very special occasion for us," she said with a smile, leaning into Alan.

He put his arm around her waist and nodded. "We really wanted to be alone tonight."

"Oohhhhhhh," Lila sang, her eyes twinkling and her finger wagging. "Friends indeed! Do I hear wedding bells?"

Pam scrambled for something to say to get rid of the couple without embarrassing Alan further. "I guess you could say it was the idea of wedding bells that brought us to Fort Myers, right, Alan?"

He hesitated only a few seconds. "Oh...right."

Lila laughed delightedly. "Dingdong, dingdong." Her head bounced left, then right.

Pam tingled at the intimacy and awkwardness of the conversation. Thankfully, their name was called and they said a hasty goodbye.

"*Talk* about dingdongs," Alan muttered as they followed a waiter to their table.

"They're harmless," she said, waving off his concern.

"They should be somewhere playing shuffleboard instead of scaring up entertainment for a nude-beach matinee," he said as he held out her chair.

The waiter handed them their menus, took their wine order and left.

Pam laughed and opened her menu. "Percy," she said.

"What?"

"Your middle name—Percy?"

He scoffed and rolled his eyes. "No."

"Pendleton?"

"No."

"Pernicious?"

He laughed. "No. Forget it—I'm not telling you."

"Will you tell me if I guess it?"

He dropped his gaze to his menu. "Sure, because you'll never guess it."

"Pembroke?"

"No—and that's enough."

"Who knows it?"

"Only my parents and siblings—and they're sworn to secrecy."

"Jo doesn't even know?"

"Nope. What looks good?"

Pam bit her tongue to keep from saying that he looked mighty tasty. "Probably the orange roughy."

"Fried, of course."

"Of course."

"How about lobster?"

Pam winced at the price. "I don't think the gift certificate will cover lobster."

"Screw the certificate—last night I slept through dinner,

and the night before I had a roll of breath mints in jail." He folded the menu and gave it a light smack. "I'm having lobster."

She watched as Alan craned his neck, looking all around. "Our waiter said he'd be right back," she reminded him.

"I know—I'm making sure they didn't seat us near a bunch of kids. I specifically asked for no kids."

"Relax—I don't see any kids."

"They can hide," he assured her, lifting the tablecloth for a peek.

"The 'P' stands for 'paranoid,'" she declared.

"Would you stop with the 'P' stuff already?"

"Alan, kids have to eat, too."

"Fine—as long as they're not sitting near me. Nearly every time Jo and I—" He stopped and a strange look came over his face. "There I go again."

Pam's heart twisted at the hurt that flashed in his eyes. "Alan, you have a lot of history with Jo—you can talk about her. Nearly every time you and Jo what?" Jo had divulged that her and Alan's sex life had been practically nonexistent, so she was relatively sure he wasn't going to say something too personal. Because of Jo's comments, Pam had always labeled Alan as a wet fish, but now she was doubting her best friend's judgment.

He straightened, but his cheer seemed forced. "Nearly every time Jo and I ate out, it seemed like some spoiled kid would ruin it—screaming, throwing food." He passed his hand over his face and a dry laugh escaped his mouth. "Now I'm wondering if things were going sour between us, and I was simply looking for any excuse to explain the awkwardness."

"What's so bad about kids anyway?" she asked.

He opened his mouth to answer, then looked puzzled. "I don't know—they're loud—"

"I'm loud."

"And messy—"

"I'm messy."

"And the diapers—"

"Okay, you got me there," she said with a grin.

"Do you like kids?" he asked, his eyebrows raised in surprise.

Pam shrugged. "I practically raised my kid sister."

"I didn't know you had a kid sister."

Pride swelled in her chest every time she thought of Dinah. "She's ten years younger—twenty-two. I sent her to *your* high school, except I made sure she finished," she added with a laugh.

"Where is she now?"

"Finishing up at Notre Dame," she said with satisfaction. "But she'll probably start law school this fall."

Alan whistled low. "Not bad."

"Well, I wanted to make sure one of the Kaminskis ended up successful and on the right side of the law," she said, thinking about her thuggy brothers.

"You're doing all right for yourself," Alan said. "Top sales producer for the largest realty company in Savannah."

Pam tingled under his praise, but knew that no matter what her achievements, she was, and would always be, a Kaminski. Dinah had informed her she would not be coming back to Savannah to practice, and Pam suspected the blight on the family name had influenced her decision. Looking across the table at a man whose name alone put him out of her reach, Pam suddenly felt queasy.

"Will you order for me?" she asked, then excused herself to the ladies' room, telling herself she had to banish the ridiculous thoughts that galloped through her head every time she looked at Alan.

In the rest room, she splashed cold water on her neck,

then pondered the wisdom of leaving Alan in Fort Myers and returning to Savannah early. Once she was back in her normal surroundings, these crazy feelings for Alan would evaporate. She could fabricate something about being needed at her office, and make her getaway. The fact that she didn't want to leave him was frightening enough to cinch her decision. She left the ladies' room feeling sad but resolute.

On the way back to the table, a male voice stopped her. "We *must* stop meeting like this, Pamela."

She turned to find Enrico dressed in black slacks and a shiny red shirt. Annoyance fueled her temper. "I can't stop to chat—I need to get back to my table."

His smile was slow and syrupy as he fell in step beside her. "Did your husband bring you or has he abandoned you once again?"

"No," Pam said through clenched teeth as she walked. "We're having a quiet, romantic dinner." But he followed her around the corner, where she came up short.

Alan stood by their table, sharing a deep kiss with Robin the computer lady.

9

SEVERAL SECONDS PASSED before Alan registered the fact that Robin, who had appeared from nowhere, was kissing him very hard and very invasively. After he managed to untangle his tongue from hers, he clasped her arms and gently pushed her away. Her eyes held the slight glaze of drunkenness. "Robin," he said with a little laugh, "I don't think this is the place."

"Oh? Then how about here?" she slurred, yanking his waistband hard. The button on his fly popped off and flipped up in the air.

A gasp sounded behind him. "Alan, how could you?" He wheeled to see Lila and Cheek standing near him, being led to a table. Lila stood with her hand over her heart. "I thought you were going to propose to Pamela tonight."

"Prrrropose?"

Alan turned the opposite direction, toward Enrico's rolling voice. The dark-haired man stood just a few steps away, with a possessive hand on Pamela's waist. Alan frowned. Where had *he* come from?

Enrico's expression was black as he stared at Pam. "I thought the two of you were already married!" Pam looked at Alan. Her mouth opened and closed, but no sound came out.

"Married?" Robin yelped, jerking his attention back to her. "I thought she was your sister!"

"Sister?" Lila shrieked, and he swung his head back to

see the older woman's face twisted in distaste. "That's disgusting."

Cheek appeared slightly less distraught. "Well, it's illegal anyway."

Everyone started talking at once, and Robin advanced on him, her eyes narrowed, and her steps wobbly. "Alan, what the hell is going on?"

Alan held up his hands. "Wait a minute. *Wait a minute!*" The group quieted. He took a deep breath and a step backward, then fell over a potted fern, landing on his tailbone hard enough to set his glasses askew. The waiter hurried over to help him up, but Alan, clawing the air in frustration, brushed him off. He scrambled to his feet, straightened his clothes, then made chopping motions in the air to punctuate his point.

"Look...you...you *people!* Pamela and I came to have a nice, quiet Valentine's Day dinner." He felt a vein bulging at his temple. "The nature of our relationship is nobody's business!" He yanked up his pants by his sagging waistband. "Now, I'll thank everyone to move along!"

Lila and Cheek were the first to bustle away, then Robin and Enrico slipped off in the same direction. Alan had the brief thought that the two of them should get together, then he looked at Pam and swept an arm awkwardly toward the table. "Shall we?"

She nodded, then stooped and picked up his wayward button. She handed it to him, then moved stiffly to her place at the table. After pulling out her chair, Alan reclaimed his seat, snapping the napkin before settling it over his lap. For several long minutes, they toyed with their wineglasses and fingered the silverware.

Although he couldn't fathom why, Alan felt as if he owed Pam an explanation. When he could stand the silence no longer, he cleared his throat. "I wasn't kissing her, you know."

"Not that it matters," she said, sipping the wine that had been served in her absence. "But the lipstick on your mouth, nose, ear and eyelid proves otherwise."

He swiped the napkin across his face, frowning at the reddish stain that transferred. "I mean I wasn't kissing her *back.*"

"Like I said, it doesn't matter."

"I guess not," he conceded with a wave, "since you were skulking in the hall with your Latin lover."

She frowned. "My lover? Where on earth did you get that idea?"

His heart lifted a notch. "You haven't been messing around with him?"

Pam rolled her eyes. "If I wanted to mess around with him, why would I have told him you and I were married?"

Unexplained relief flooded through him. "And he believed it?"

"Crazy, huh?" she asked with a little laugh. "That someone would think we were husband and wife?"

"Yeah," he said, joining her laughter. "Ridiculous."

"I mean, you and me—" Pam's giggles escalated.

"Right," he said, laughing harder. *"Mr. and Mrs. Alan Parish."*

She roared. *"P-Pamela P-Parish!"*

Alan wiped his eyes and took a big gulp of wine. "The way the last couple of days have been going, I suppose anything seems possible."

"It's been an adventure," she agreed.

He sighed and glanced across the table, struck anew by her glowing beauty. Pam looked like a movie star, her hair and skin wrought with gold, her mouth wide, her eyes shining. Her gaze met his and Alan's ears started ringing. He felt as if he were teetering on the edge of a precipice, in danger of falling into a pit so deep he might never return. The notion skating through his mind, the emotion blooming in his chest was nothing short of insanity. He was falling for Pamela Kaminski.

Pam's smile evaporated and she squirmed in her chair. Looking into her glass, she said, "I was thinking about leaving tomorrow."

Alan stopped and choked on the wine in his throat. "Leaving? You mean, going back to Savannah?"

She nodded.

He experienced the panicky feeling that something wonderful was about to slip through his fingers. "B-but why?"

Pam abandoned her glass and rolled her eyes heavenward, counting on her beautifully manicured fingers. "A bad flight, a flat tire, a dilapidated hotel, a powder blue limo, a police record..." Her voice trailed off. "You came to the beach for a week of R&R," she said. "And so far it's been more like a week of S&M."

"Well, it hasn't been your fault," he offered generously. But she simply smirked.

"Not totally," he added weakly.

"Lying is not one of your talents."

Spotting an opening, he leaned forward with eyebrows raised. "Is that a concession that I have talents elsewhere?"

"No."

Deflated, he sat back. "Oh."

Surprised at the wounded look on his face, Pam scrambled to soothe his hurt feelings. "I mean, I wouldn't know if you had talents elsewhere..." She swallowed and searched for firmer footing. "It's not like Jo and I ever discussed your, uh...anything."

He shifted in his seat. "Well, I should hope not."

"Oh, no," she assured him hurriedly. "Jo and I never talked about what you and she did—or *didn't* do."

Alan pursed his lips. "Didn't do?"

A flush burned her neck on its way up. "I didn't say 'didn't.'"

"Yes, you did."

Panic fluttered in her stomach. "Well, I didn't *mean* 'didn't.' I meant...oh, damn."

He closed his eyes and downed the rest of his wine. After setting his empty glass on the table with a thunk, he inhaled deeply. "So, Jo wasn't happy with our sex life."

Pam shook her head. "She *never* said that."

He flagged the waiter for more wine, then gave her a dry laugh. "Well, I have to admit we didn't exactly keep the sheets ablaze."

She held up her hands. "I don't want to hear this."

"I can't explain it. Jo is a beautiful woman, but when it came to—"

Pam put her hands over her ears and started to hum, but she could still read his lips, and what she saw made her squeeze her eyes shut. "I'm not listening," she sang. "I'm noooooooooooooot liiiiiisssstennnnniiiiing. I'm noooooooooooooot liiiiiisssstennnnniiiiing. I'm noooooooooooooot liiiiiisssstennnnniiiiing." When she opened her eyes, Alan sat staring at her, along with two waiters who stood by the table, their arms loaded with trays. She smiled sheepishly, straightened her napkin, then gestured for them to serve.

During dinner, neither she nor Alan mentioned the subject of her returning to Savannah early. They talked about their respective jobs, mutual acquaintances and state politics. They talked about the Braves and the Hawks and the Falcons, one advantage of having sports-minded brothers, she noted. They laughed and argued and laughed some more, and Pam hated to see the pleasant meal come to an end.

For dessert, they decided to split a rich, velvety cheese-cake with cinnamon topping, which reminded Pam of the unused bottle of body liqueur in their room.

She picked up her utensil and with every luscious bite, she imagined devouring him—biting, licking and swallowing him whole. She savored every succulent bite, allowing the sweetness to melt on her tongue before letting it slide down her throat. The more she ate, the more moist her flimsy panties grew until she nearly moaned aloud. At the sound of Alan's chuckle, she glanced up, afraid she had. Instead, he was simply watching her.

"Was it good?"

"Wonderful," she said, smiling to herself.

"You're killing me," he said, shifting in his seat.

She frowned. "What do you mean?"

"Pam," he said, leaning close and lowering his voice. "Do you always eat dessert with a knife?"

With a start, she stared at the huge, blunt dinner knife in her hand. She glanced up with a sheepish smile, enormously relieved to see the roving Italian musicians were approaching their table.

The men were dressed in brilliant costumes of red, black and gold, with snow-white shirts. The violinist nodded to Alan and kissed Pam's hand, then put his instrument to his shoulder and began to play a sweet, haunting melody, accompanied by the other musicians.

It was almost too much for her—the great food, the good wine, the beautiful music...and Alan's company. She glanced over at him and inhaled sharply at the desire she saw in his blue eyes. He abandoned his napkin, stood and swept his hand toward the tiny vacant area by their table. "May I have this dance?" Then he leaned forward and whispered conspiratorially, "Of course, I'll have to hold you close to keep my pants up."

She grinned, then accepted his hand and allowed him to pull her into his arms for a slow waltz. He was a surprisingly good dancer, with natural rhythm and perfect form. It was a good thing he could lead, she decided with her chin resting on his shoulder, because she was too weak-kneed to do little more than follow. He smelled wonderfully spicy and she ached to taste the skin on his neck. He melded her body to his until she felt every muscle beneath his clothing. They might have been the only two people in the universe. When the music ended, she sensed his reluctance to part was as strong as hers, but with an audience, they had little choice. While the other diners applauded, Alan raised her hand and kissed her fingertips.

"Happy Valentine's Day," he whispered.

Later, on the way back to the hotel, Pam was quiet, consumed by raging desire for the man next to her, yet lamenting the ramifications of her actions. Conversely, Alan seemed downright cheerful, whistling tunelessly under his breath and fidgeting with all the gadgets on the limousine panel until she was ready to scream. The walk from the parking lot to their door seemed interminably long to her.

"Couldn't get that room Linda had reserved, huh?" Pam said, laughing to hide her nervousness as she stepped through the door onto the familiar shag carpet.

"Actually," Alan said with a smile, "I told her I'd changed my mind since we only have two more nights. Want to go down to the beach for a walk?"

Remembering the disastrous results of their last moonlit stroll, she shook her head.

"How about the hot tub?" he asked.

"I'm not fainthearted, Alan, but even *I* am not brave

enough to climb into that algae-infested wading pool. Besides, Cheek might be in it, naked.''

"Which could account for the algae," he said. "Then let's make our own hot tub."

She laughed. "What?"

He gestured toward the bathroom. "That ridiculous tub in there—it's plenty big enough if we fill it up with hot water."

Amazed at the change in his demeanor, she reached up and lifted his glasses. "Who are you and what have you done with Alan P.—the-'P'-stands-for-tight-as-a-pin—Parish?"

His mouth quirked to the side. "You better get your bathing suit before he comes back."

Pam looked into his blue eyes and studied his boyish face. He was so incredibly handsome…and had turned into such a surprise. Ignoring the warning flags that sprang up en masse at the periphery of her brain, she grinned and said, "I'll meet you in the deep end."

She grabbed her suit, went into the bathroom, then turned on the hot water, unable to ignore the pounding of her heart. Biting her lip hard, she stared at herself in the mirror as she tucked her curves into the gold bikini that had sparked a light in Alan's eyes at the department store. Beneath the harsh illumination of the bare bulb in the room, she looked raw and vulnerable. Her eyes stung from indecision. She wanted Alan so much her chest hurt. "If this is wrong," she whispered, "send me a sign."

The bulb popped, then went dark with a sizzling sound.

She stood in the dark for several seconds, then said, "I need to be really, really sure. Would you mind sending another sign?"

"Pam?" Alan knocked lightly on the door. "Who are you talking to?"

"Uh, no one," she yelled. "The light went out."

His chuckle reverberated through the door. "I'll get the Elvis candles you bought."

Pam looked heavenward. "I gave it my best shot."

He was back within a few seconds, wearing trunks and bearing matches. She placed "Love Me Tender" candles around the room strategically, growing increasingly alarmed at the romantic atmosphere they were creating. She lowered herself into the hot water just as Alan reappeared with a bottle. "Ta-dah!"

"Champagne?"

He uncorked the bottle, spilling foam on the pink tile. "Since I didn't get a drop at the wedding reception, I gave Twiggy fifty bucks to find a bottle of my favorite. Happy Valentine's Day." Alan handed her a full glass, then stepped into the water, only to jump back out. "Good Lord, Pam! Are you cooking shrimp in there?"

Already light-headed at the sight of the candlelight dancing on his sleek, muscled chest, she sipped the champagne and giggled as the bubbles went up her nose. "Ease in, Alan, you'll get used to it."

He tried again, gasping and wincing, sending her into fits of laughter as he squatted into the water inch by inch. "It's a good thing I don't like kids," he muttered as he settled in up to his armpits. "Because my sperm have been parboiled."

"Is that what the 'P' stands for?"

"Cute, real cute."

"Is it 'Parker'?"

"No."

"Preston?"

"No."

"Palmer?"

"No! Enough already. Either turn on the cold water or the egg timer because I'll be done in a few minutes."

Pam turned on the cold water to let it drip. "What's the big deal about your middle name?" She started as his leg brushed against hers beneath the water.

"It's private," he said with a smile. His leg brushed hers again, and she nearly groaned with the desire that welled within her. "Don't you have something private, something you don't share with everyone?"

She manufactured a laugh. "Private? You forget who you're talking to. My life has been public property in Savannah since I was sixteen. Don't tell me you haven't heard the stories."

"I have," he admitted, raking his gaze over her. "But I'm not sure how many of the stories are true and how many of them are pure fantasy on the part of the men who told them."

Her neck felt rubbery, so she laid her head back and looked at him through slitted eyelids. "Alan, have *you* ever fantasized about me?"

His eyes widened and he cleared his throat, then drained his champagne glass. Pam's skin tingled in anticipation.

"I've always thought you were beautiful, Pam," he said finally, moving lower in the water and settling his leg against the length of hers. "But I've never fantasized about you."

She pressed her lips together in disappointment. He wasn't attracted to her, after all. The sexual current she'd felt between them had been a figment of her teenage imagination, dating back to the time when she'd dreamed that Alan P. Parish would notice her, ask her out, take her to his fine home—

"Until this week," he added quietly.

Pam lifted her head.

"I know what you think of me, Pam—that I'm an automaton, a computer geek—"

"A tight-ass," she added with a smile.

He smirked. "Thanks." Then he moved closer, and set her glass aside with his. He floated inches over her in the water before lowering himself against her, setting the warm water into motion. "But I'm not a machine, Pam."

His face was only inches from hers, and she felt his breath fan her cheek. The water lapped around them, warming her skin, then falling away to leave her covered with goose bumps. Her nipples hardened. His proximity crowded her senses and she had never felt so close to losing control. "Are you sure? Because I—I can certainly feel your hard drive."

"I want you."

Pam closed her eyes, trying to recall any shred of relief she had felt the morning after their near lapse on the beach, any rationalization that she shouldn't be feeling like this. But now his hands on her obliterated all doubts, negated all concerns, neutralized all complications. And her hands moved of their own volition to the nape of her neck to loosen the ties of her bikini top. She allowed the water to float the material away from her breasts, and Alan crushed her against him, claiming her mouth in a plundering kiss.

Pam raised her body to meet his and he clasped her urgently, squeezing her hips against his, whispering her name into her throat. After a thorough exploration of her mouth, he set aside his fogged glasses and drew back to view her breasts.

"You are magnificent." The sheer wonder in his voice sent waves of desire flooding her limbs. He dragged her breath from her lungs by pulling a puckered nipple into his mouth.

"Oh, Alan." She pushed her fingers through his hair and

arched into him, urging him to take as much of her into his mouth as possible. His erection strained against her thigh, and she ran her hands down his neck, over his muscled back, and under the waistband of his trunks.

Their moans echoed off the walls of the small room and Pam had never felt so aroused. The combination of the heated water, the candlelight and the man were incredibly erotic. Every nerve ending, every muscle, every sense burned and throbbed with raw desire and she raked her hands over his body. His name emerged from her throat over and over, as if some part of her suspected their time together was short and she wanted to experience as much of him as possible.

He devoured her, drawing on her breasts one at a time, rolling her sensitized nipples between his finger and thumb. His hands skated over her body, assuming the rhythm of the water until their movements became so frenzied, the now-lukewarm water splashed over the edges and onto the tile.

Alan felt his body growing more engorged, yearning for release. The feelings she had unleashed in him were so staggering, he prayed he could maintain control long enough to please her. "Let's go to bed," he said thickly against her neck and she moaned her agreement.

He drew back and tried to stand, fell, and succeeded in dunking them both before they gained their footing. Pam stopped long enough to grab a towel for her sopping hair. The sight of her standing bare-breasted was enough to make him grit his teeth.

"We'd better hurry," he said, tugging on her hand.

They slipped and slid across the tiled floor, laughing and cursing until they crossed the threshold of the bedroom. They tumbled onto the bed, launching a small tidal wave. Alan kicked off his trunks and rolled down her bikini bottoms, groaning when he uncovered the nest of wet blond curls between her firm, tanned thighs. He raised himself above her, pushing her wet hair back from her face. "You are so beautiful," he whispered hoarsely. "I need to make love to you now—are you protected?"

She nodded, her blue eyes luminous, her luscious upside-down mouth soft and swollen. With utmost restraint, he lowered himself, rubbing his straining shaft against her. Oh so carefully, he probed her wetness, then sank inside her slowly, capturing her mouth with his and absorbing her gasps as their bodies melded.

Heaven. She felt like pure heaven around him, pulsing, kneading, drawing his life fluid to the surface much too quickly. He slowed and clenched his teeth, wanting their lovemaking to last, postponing the moment she would pull away from him. For now he wanted to be inside her, wrapped around her, smelling her, tasting her. When he found a slow rhythm, she began to pant beneath him, clawing as his back. He was so stunned at the level of her response, he was momentarily distracted from his own building release and concentrated on making her climax powerful.

He laved her earlobe and whispered erotic words he'd never uttered before, phrases loosened from his tongue by the fantasy woman writhing beneath him. He moved with her, responding to every moan and gasp with more intense probing until her cries escalated and she climaxed around him, her contracting muscles finally breaking his restraint and unleashing the most intense orgasm he'd ever experienced. They rode out the vestiges of their explosive pleasure, slowing to a languid grind. At last they stilled, but the water mattress bumped them against each other, eliciting gasps as their tender flesh met.

He gingerly lifted himself from her and rolled to spoon

her against him, half to hold her close for a while longer, half to avoid facing her until he had time to sort out a few things for himself. The regrets, the remorse, the self-recrimination had not yet set in, and for the time being, he simply wanted to enjoy the intimacy of lying with this wonderful creature, however fleeting the time might be.

Alan sighed and closed his eyes, pushing his nose into her damp hair, inhaling her scent. He couldn't remember feeling more content, but he blamed his thoughts of spending the rest of his nights like this on the fog of sleep that ebbed over him. His dreams were restless, fraught with stress-packed, nerve-shattering days of living with Pamela Kaminski.

10

WHEN PAM'S EYES popped open, the first light of dawn had found its way between the heavy opaque curtains over the window and sliding glass door. Despite the sunny warmth, a cold blanket of dread descended over her. She craned her neck slowly toward the mirrored ceiling, muttering words of denial until she was faced with the naked truth.

"Oh…my…God," she murmured, groaning at the tangle of bare tanned arms and legs they presented. They'd *done* it—the deed, the wild thing, the horizontal bop—they'd had *sex*. She and Alan. Her and her best friend's ex. Panic ballooned in her chest and she pushed herself up, frantically whispering, "Oh my God, oh my God, oh my God."

Alan stirred and rolled to his back, displaying a pup-tent erection beneath the thin sheet. She averted her eyes, cursed the erotic scenes that kept replaying in her head and began to extricate herself from his grasp as gently as possible.

"Hey," he mumbled in complaint, pulling her against him.

She punched his arm. "Let me go," she protested, scrambling to get out of the rolling bed.

"You really should work on that morning disposition," he muttered with a yawn.

She bent and scooped a towel from the floor, which she wrapped around herself. Astounded at his nonchalance, she bounced a pillow off his face. "Get up! Can't you see we're in big trouble here?"

He blinked and sat up, shaking his head as if to clear it, then swung his feet to the floor. "Excuse me?"

"Alan, we had sex last night."

"I was there—or don't you remember?" he asked wryly, standing for a full-body stretch.

That was the problem—she remembered his mind-blowing participation all too well. Pam glanced down at his raging morning erection, then expelled an explosive sigh. "Put a towel on that rack, would you?"

She tossed him a pillowcase they had somehow managed to work free during their lovemaking, then jammed her hands on her hips. "*What* are we going to do now?"

Holding the crumpled cloth over his privates, Alan scrubbed his hand over his face, then ventured, "Go to Walt Disney World?"

"That's not even remotely funny," she snapped.

"Could I have a few seconds to wake up? And maybe relieve myself?"

It had meant nothing to him, she realized with a jolt. And why should it? He wasn't the one who would have to face Jo on a regular basis when they returned home. In fact, from a man's point of view, sleeping with the best friend of the woman who had ditched him at the altar was probably the most perfect revenge he could exact. Hurt stabbed her deep, and she felt like a fool for not seeing the situation so clearly last night. Pam swept her hand toward the bathroom. "Be my guest," she said with as much indifference as she could muster.

When he had closed the door, she strode to the closet, yanked out her large canvas beach bag and started stuffing her personal articles inside. Most of the clothes she could leave here, she decided—since Alan had bought them, he could dispose of them however he wished.

Not relishing another plane ride so soon after their turbulent experience a few days ago, she decided that the bus sounded like the best alternative home—even if it took two days, which she presumed it would. Today was Thursday, so she'd still be back in Savannah by late Friday, or Saturday at the latest. Which would give her plenty of time to decide what—or if—she was going to tell Jo.

She jammed her Elvis paraphernalia into the bag and practiced her speech. "Gee, Jo, you were finished with him and he was just so darned sexy. No, I promise we weren't sleeping together behind your back while you and Alan were an item."

"Pam."

Alan's voice sounded behind her, jangling her already clanging nerves so badly she dropped the bag, and her towel with it. Yanking the towel back in place, she wheeled to find Alan leaning on the doorjamb.

"What are you doing?" he asked quietly.

She retrieved the bag and continued rooting through the tiny closet. "What does it look like I'm doing? I'm packing."

"To go home? Why?"

She turned and leveled her gaze on him.

He did, at least, have the grace to blush. "I mean, I can guess why, but I don't think this is the best way to handle what just happened, do you?"

"You have a better plan?"

Alan shrugged. "Try not to blow it out of proportion. I was lonely, you were lonely. We had a romantic evening—everyone treated us as a couple. We drank half a bottle of wine, then topped it off with good champagne."

He looked contrite. "I owe you an apology—I feel guilty as hell for dragging you down here, and now…"

"Now look at the fine mess we've made," she finished for him, ending with a sigh. "There's no need to apologize, Alan. You didn't exactly hold a gun to my head."

He pressed his lips together in a tight line. "Sleeping together wasn't particularly smart, considering the touchy circumstances, but we're adults and surely we can exercise enough control to make sure it doesn't happen again."

"Oh, it can *never* happen again," she said emphatically.

"Agreed," he said, walking to stop an arm's length away from her. "Since we have that settled, now you can stay."

"It's not settled, Alan," she said, dropping her gaze. "What am I going to tell Jo?"

"*We,*" he said firmly, "aren't going to tell Jo anything. She's married, Pam. She doesn't care about my sex life— or yours. And even if she did, it's none of her business."

"But how will I face her?"

"As if nothing happened," he said simply, affirming her earlier suspicion that their lovemaking had shaken her far more than it had affected him.

"But I can't lie to her, Alan. She's my best friend."

He lifted his hands. "Fine—if we get home and Jo asks you, 'Pam, did you and Alan sleep together?,' you can say, 'Yes, as a matter of fact, Jo, we did.'"

"It would never occur to Jo to ask," Pam said with a wry smile.

"My point exactly," he said. "But you might arouse her curiosity if you went scurrying home early." He gave her a lopsided smile. "So put down your bag and I promise to stay out of your way until Saturday. Hopefully we can still go home as friends."

He made it sound so simple—they had made a mistake, and they wouldn't do it again. Period. That was Alan—Mr.

Practical. She lifted a corner of her mouth. Maybe that's what the 'P' stood for. Even though he obviously wasn't wrestling with the same troubling issues their lovemaking had unearthed in her psyche, perhaps he was right. Maybe they needed a couple of days to get back on a casual footing. Although she would never look at Alan in quite the same way, it would be a shame to lose his friendship because she simply couldn't cope with their lapse.

"I'll stay," she said lightly. "And of course we'll go home as friends." She dropped the bag and gave him her brightest smile. "I'll go shopping today, and do some sightseeing."

"And I'll find something to do," he said. "And if you're out late—"

"—or if you're out late..."

"—we'll see each other..."

"—tomorrow," she finished.

He nodded. "Fine."

She nodded. "Fine."

"Do you want to shower first?"

"Sure," she said, and walked past him. The pink-tiled room did not seem nearly so electric this morning, although the vestiges of their interlude were scattered throughout: her bikini top, the burnt-down candles, the half-empty bottle of champagne. She closed her eyes for a few seconds and squashed the mushrooming regret when it threatened to overwhelm her.

"By the way," Alan said behind her.

She whirled to see him squinting at her from the open doorway, just as something crunched under her foot.

"Have you seen my glasses?"

Pam looked down, picked up her foot, then winced and nodded.

ALAN PUSHED his glasses higher on his nose, frowning when he encountered the bulky piece of masking tape that held the broken bridge of his frames together. He sank lower in the upholstered seat of the nearly empty movie theater and smirked at the corny previews. With a sigh he glanced at the vacant seat next to him and imagined Pam sitting there, munching popcorn and giggling like a teenager.

It was funny how much his perception of her had changed in the last few days. She was still the sexy bombshell who made him a little nervous, but now...now he had glimpsed the warm, funny, smart woman who lurked beneath the showy facade. Sure, her showy side inflamed his baser needs, but it was her squeal of laughter when they'd ridden the Wave Runner and her shining face when he'd filled the moat of her sand castle that stayed with him every waking minute.

The ear-numbing, teeth-jarring, bone-melting, mind-blowing sex was simply a bonus.

He smiled a slow, lazy grin. The sex was a big, fat cherry on top of a sundae more delectable than any he could have imagined as a kid. Which presented an interesting paradox, he noted as the main feature bounced onto the screen. If Pamela Kaminski was such a catch, what was keeping him from pursuing her with gusto?

He imagined Pam counting off the reasons on her brightly colored fingernails. "Because my friendship with your ex-fiancée means more to me than any relationship we could ever have, Alan. Because I have dozens of men waiting for my return, Alan. And most important, because you're not the kind of guy I'd settle for, Alan."

The flick started, a splashy good-guys bad-guys film with several gorgeous women and just enough one-liners to make it amusing. But his mind wandered from the movie plot to Pamela so often, he lost track of which double agent crossed which federal bureau so when the movie credits rolled, he wasn't quite sure what had happened or who had gotten the girl. But he had the sinking feeling it wouldn't be him.

He sat through another matinee he couldn't follow, at the end of which he had to admit that for the first time in his thirty-odd years, he was completely consumed with, distracted by and besotted over a woman. A woman who was beyond his reach.

When he walked outside, he squinted into the light, even though dusk was already falling. Oh well, he thought as he joined the mingling crowd on the sidewalk, things would be different when they got back to Savannah. He would return to his demanding job running his consulting business, and she would return to the frantic pace of real-estate sales, along with her bottomless pool of boyfriends. They would probably see each other occasionally at charity functions. He would wave and she would smile, and no one would ever know they had made passionate love in a gaudy room in Fort Myers on Valentine's Day.

Determined to stay away from the beachfront area to avoid running into Robin, Alan strolled along the retail district, browsing in music and electronics stores. He wandered by a jewelry-store window and stopped when he spotted a gold sand-castle pendant. He desperately wanted to give Pam something to remember him by, and the pendant seemed to call him. He walked inside and left fifteen minutes later with the pendant and a matching gold chain. He wasn't sure when or if he'd give it to her, but for now, buying the pendant seemed like the right thing to do.

He bought a couple of CD's by local artists, then stopped at a sports bar and ordered a sandwich and a beer. The ponytailed bartender who served him found a Georgia State basketball game on one of the many TV screens and made small talk while he washed glass mugs.

The barkeep wore a tight T-shirt with the sleeves ripped off to show his many tattoos to their best advantage. Alan tried not to stare, but he must have failed because the guy quirked a bushy eyebrow and asked, "You ever had a tattoo?"

Alan shook his head and pointed to one on the man's arm, squinting. "Is that an ad?"

"Yep—best tattoo parlor in town is just down the street. I get a discount for wearing the ad."

"Human billboards," Alan acknowledged with a tip of his bottle. "Now *there's* an untapped industry." He figured he must be getting a buzz because the idea of someone selling their skin to advertisers, inch by inch, actually sounded plausible. In which case, Pam's body would be worth a fortune, he noted dryly, wondering how much her cleavage would command on the open market. *Location, location, location.*

The bartender leaned on the bar and asked, "Hey, man, are you busy later tonight?"

Alan frowned and deepened his voice. "You're barking up the wrong tree, fella."

"Huh?" The bartender pulled back, then scoffed. "Nah, man, my girlfriend's swinging by and bringing a friend with her. You like redheads?"

"Sure, but—"

"Great! Her name's Pru."

"Thanks anyway, but I'm really not—"

"Saaaaaaaaay." Something past Alan's shoulder had obviously claimed the man's attention. "I could go for some of that," the bartender whispered in a husky voice.

Alan turned on his stool to see Pamela walking toward the bar wearing an outfit of walking shorts and sleeveless sweater that would have been unremarkable on ninety-nine percent of the female population. She seemed intent on finding something in her purse and hadn't spotted him yet. If Alan had been quick—and motivated—he could have thrown some cash on the bar and left. But his reflexes were a little delayed, he conceded, and the sheer pleasure of seeing her after spending the day apart disintegrated his thoughts of leaving.

When she looked up, she did a double take and stopped midstride, then approached him with a wary expression on her face. "Small world," he offered along with a smile. He patted the stool next to him. "Have a seat—I'll buy you a beer."

She leaned one firm hip against the stool and gestured vaguely. "Thanks anyway—I actually came in to find a pay phone. My cell-phone battery died in the middle of a conversation with Mrs. Wingate."

"Is she ready to buy the Sheridan house?"

"Not yet—she's got a priest over there now consecrating the flower beds."

"Don't let me keep you."

"That's all right," she said with a wave. "She probably took getting cut off as some kind of omen and might not come to the phone anyway." Pam glanced at the bartender. "Nice artwork," she said, nodding toward his colorful arms.

Wearing a wolfish grin, the man flexed his biceps and leaned toward Pam. "Thanks."

Jealousy barbed through Alan and he glared at the beefy man. "Pam, what did you do all day?"

She told him about her day of sight-seeing. "There are some beautiful homes here and over on Sanibel Island," she declared. "The real-estate market seems to be very strong—lots of money to be made."

He bit the inside of his cheek as a disturbing thought struck him. "You're not thinking about moving?"

"Not here," she said. "Even though I like it. I always thought Atlanta would be nice—I have lots of friends there."

So she had lovers all over the state, he mused. "Atlanta's a fun city."

She nodded and brushed a lock of hair behind her ear—the ear in which he'd murmured unmentionables only last night. "As long as my mother is alive, I guess I'll stay in Savannah."

"I can't imagine the state my mother will be in by the time I return," Alan said with a wry grin.

"She liked Jo, didn't she?"

He nodded and peeled off the curling corner of the label on his beer bottle. "She thought Jo would make an excellent wife and hostess, an asset to my career."

"She doesn't want grandchildren?"

"My sister has two kids, and my mother thinks that's plenty enough people in this world to call her Granny."

Pam giggled. "Mom doesn't have grandkids—that we know of. Of course, knowing my brothers, who knows how many Kaminskis could be running around."

Alan laughed and tipped his bottle for another drink. Every family, rich or poor, had its dysfunction. "Have you had dinner?"

"I'm not really very hungry," she said, dropping her gaze again. "Thanks anyway. I'm tired—I think I'll get back to the hotel and turn in early."

Their eyes met and the reason behind her fatigue hung in the air between them. Alan gripped the bottle hard to keep from reaching for her. "Ah, come on," he said. "Why don't you stay for a beer—what's one beer between friends?"

The corners of her uneven mouth turned up slowly, then she relented with a nod. "Okay, one beer."

ALAN STARTED AWAKE, then winced at the sour taste in his mouth. But the movement of his facial muscles sent an explosion of pain to his temples and he groaned aloud, which sounded like a gong in his ears. He closed his eyes and waited until most of the pain and noise subsided before attempting to put two thoughts together.

He was in the hotel room, and he could hear Pam's snore beside him, so it appeared they had slept in the same bed. Straining, he remembered they had consumed large quantities of beer and had left the sports bar, but that's when his memory failed him. Had they gone directly back to the room? And then what?

He opened his eyes one at a time in the early-morning light and gingerly reached up to adjust his broken glasses, which were somehow still on his face. He moved his head to see the reflection in the ceiling. Another gonging groan escaped him when he saw they were indeed naked and intimately entwined.

Not again.

Pam lay on her stomach and the sheet had fallen down to expose the rub-on rose tattoo on her tanned hip. When his scrutiny triggered inappropriate responses beneath his half of the sheet, he pulled himself up a millimeter at a time and stumbled to the bathroom in search of a glass of water.

His hip ached from the unaccustomed lusty exercise, and he rubbed it as he downed the water. But at the sharp tenderness of his skin, he turned to glance in the mirror and smiled dryly. He must have been blitzed because he'd allowed Pam to rub one of her fake tattoos on *his* hip. A wet washcloth and a little soap would take care of it, he figured.

Except when he scrubbed at the tattoo, the pain increased and the stubborn design refused to budge. "I must be allergic to the dye," he muttered, and scrubbed harder. But minutes later when he lifted the cloth and saw the tattoo still had not faded, terror twisted his stomach.

"No," he said frantically. "It can't be real!"

He backed up to the mirror for a better look, but he couldn't make out the tattoo. Letters of some kind? It was backward in the reflection, so he snatched up Pam's hand mirror and positioned it to read the reflected word. His eyes widened and his hands started to shake.

Paaaaaaaaaaaaaaaaammmmmmmmm!

Pamela jerked awake, unable to pinpoint the origin of the invasion into her peaceful sleep. She swallowed painfully and lifted her head. The sound of breaking glass from the bathroom made her sit up. "Alan," she called, holding her head. "Are you okay?"

The door swung open and he emerged naked, his face puckered and red. "No, I am not okay. In fact, I'm about as far from okay as I've ever been!"

Pam rubbed her tender hip and grimaced. "Don't make me play twenty questions, Alan. It hurts to talk."

"You!" he bellowed, shaking his finger at her. "You talked me into it!"

She sighed. "Did we do it again?"

"Yes!" he roared. "But that's not what I'm talking about."

Her frustration peaked. "Then what *are* you talking about?"

"This!" he yelled, then turned around and pointed to his bare hip.

She leaned forward and squinted. "A tattoo? You got a tattoo?" Laughter erupted from the back of her throat. "You got a tattoo!" Then she stood, twisted to look at her own hip and squealed in delight. "No—we both got tattoos! A rose! Isn't it great?" She strode over to him and glanced down. "What does yours say?" Then she stopped and stumbled backward at the sight of the name etched on Alan's skin, enclosed in a red heart. "P-Pam's?" She covered her mouth with both hands and lifted her gaze to his.

"THERE ARE ALL KINDS of new laser procedures to remove tattoos," she assured him as they moved down the path toward the beach. Alan walked woodenly beside her, occasionally stabbing at his taped glasses.

"But I think we're skirting the bigger issue here," she continued, trotting to keep up with him, even though he was limping slightly, favoring his tender hip. "What happened last night absolutely *cannot* happen again."

"I agree," he said curtly, staring straight ahead.

"We've only got one more day and one more night, so we should be able to stay sober and keep our hands to ourselves."

"Right."

"Let's try to enjoy the time we have left," she said amiably as they stepped onto the warm white sand.

He stopped and turned to her. "How about 'Let's just try to make it through tomorrow with as few calamities as possible'?"

Pam swallowed and smiled weakly. "That's fine, too."

They rented chaise lounges and Pam couldn't help noticing that Alan waited until she had hers situated, then planted his several feet away. "Safety precaution," he said flatly, then snapped open the newspaper he'd brought to read.

Frowning, Pam turned to her own reading material and tried to blot the disturbing thoughts of Alan from her mind. She had missed him yesterday, and the realization had shaken her badly. So when she'd stumbled across him in the sports bar, she had allowed herself to be persuaded to stay for a drink because she simply wanted to spend time with him. And although the rest of the night remained fuzzy, some incidents she recalled rather clearly.

Such as the fact that she *had* been the one who suggested they get tattoos, inspired, possibly, by the bartender's impressive collection. And Alan had been hesitant, but she had dragged him down the street, and sent him into one booth while she entered another one for her design of choice. Where he'd gotten ''Pam's'' was less clear to her, and the fact that they'd made whoopee again last night only added to the confusion.

Her heart lay heavy in her chest and she tried to convince herself that things would be better once they returned to Savannah. For one thing, she would rarely see him, if at all, since their connection to each other—Jo—no longer existed. It was for the best, she knew, because she didn't want to be running into him at every turn…didn't want to be reminded of the few days they were together when names, backgrounds and at-risk relationships were irrelevant and all that mattered was the powerful sexual chemistry between them.

''Hello.''

Pam looked up and smothered a cringe when she saw Enrico standing over her chair, his lips curved into a sultry smile. Resplendent in orange nut-huggers, the man nodded toward Alan who was still hidden behind a newspaper. ''I see your man is neglecting you once again.'' He wagged his eyebrows. ''Perhaps I can remedy that situation.''

Annoyed, Pam began rummaging in her bag. ''I doubt it.''

''Could I interest you in a walk up the beach?''

She jammed on her sunglasses. ''No.''

"How about a drink?"

She lay her head back. "No."

He leaned close to her and the stench of alcohol rolled off his breath. "You like to tease, no?"

"No," Alan said behind him.

Pam lifted her head and looked up at Alan who stood with his paper under his arm, glaring at Enrico. How like a man to ignore a woman until someone else comes sniffing around. She smiled tightly. "I can handle this, Alan."

His gaze darted to her, then he lifted his hands in retreat and reclaimed his chair.

But Enrico folded his arms and followed him back to his chair. "She is not worth fighting for, *señor?*"

"That is enough," Pam declared, sitting up. "I think you'd better leave, Enrico."

Enrico stood over Alan, taking advantage of the situation. "She is too much woman for you, eh?"

Pam's patience snapped and she scrambled to her feet. "Leave, Enrico!"

He sneered and jerked a thumb toward Alan, who had risen to his feet. "Perhaps your man is weak?" Just as he lunged for Alan, Pam launched herself at the man with an angry growl, climbing his hairy back. She propelled him into Alan and they all went down in the sand. Once the breath returned to her lungs, Pam pummeled the man's back.

Sand flew as they rolled around, scrambling for leverage. Alan splayed his hand over Enrico's face and pushed him back, trying to avoid the man's swinging arms. Pam yelped, clawing the grit out of her eyes while showering Enrico with the blinding stuff. Alan rolled behind the man and grabbed him in a choke-hold. The man grabbed handfuls of sand and threw them in the air.

Somewhere in the background she heard a voice yell for

the police. Incensed, she wanted to land one good jab while Alan held him. Pam made a fist, drew back and threw the hardest punch she could through the swirling sand, eliciting a dull groan when she made contact with skin and bone.

She stepped back to blink her eyes clear. But when she massaged her throbbing knuckles in satisfaction, she saw Enrico several yards down the beach, jogging away, and he appeared unfazed by Pam's right hook.

When she glanced back to the site of the scuffle, her stomach twisted. Alan sat in the sand, glaring at her, holding his hand over his right eye.

Whatever apology she might have conjured up was cut short by the arrival of a uniformed officer. "Hello," the cop said, standing over Alan with a tight smile. "Again."

"WELL, look on the bright side," Pam said as she led the way to the double-parked limo the following morning.

Numb from another night in jail and a head full of contradicting thoughts, Alan gingerly touched his swollen right eye and asked, "And that would be?"

"We didn't have sex last night," she said brightly.

Which would have been the only redeeming event of the past twenty-four hours, Alan thought miserably.

"And we're leaving today," she sang, obviously anxious to return home. "I checked us out of the hotel—Twiggy said goodbye. I bought a suitcase and packed your things—they're in the car."

He stopped and stared at two new dents and the Kaminiskiesque parking job that left only two tires of the pimpmobile on the street, but he didn't say anything. Instead, he opened the back door of the limo and climbed in, banging the door closed behind him.

"You're letting me drive to the airport?" Pam yelled

from the driver's seat after she buzzed down the divider panel.

Alan clicked his seat belt into place, pulled the strap tight and laid his head back. "Your definition of driving is a loose interpretation, but I'm too drained to argue."

"Okay," she said excitedly, revving the engine. "I'm starved—do you mind if we stop and get something to eat on the way? We've got plenty of time before the flight."

"Go for it," he said, removing his broken glasses so he couldn't witness the driving event.

Of course, he hadn't anticipated she would attempt to take the limo through a drive-through window—they were stuck in a tight curve by a squawking monitor for forty-five minutes. No longer surprised by any stunt she pulled, Alan ordered an ice-cream sandwich to hold against his puffy eye and munched a hamburger in the back seat during the melee. When the scraping sounds became too unbearable, he turned up the TV and watched a rerun of "Laugh-In" until she finally eased the car by the metal posts and the high curbs.

She buzzed down the panel when they were on the expressway again. "We still have over an hour," she yelled cheerfully. "We'll make it."

He buzzed up the panel and unwrapped the ice-cream sandwich.

Five minutes later they were at a dead standstill. She buzzed down the panel. "It's a freaking parking lot out here—the radio says there's a tractor-trailer overturned and we won't move for at least an hour. Don't worry—we'll still make it." She smiled, then buzzed up the panel.

Alan sighed and picked up the remote control. Then a thought struck him and he buzzed down the panel. "Hey, Kaminski?"

She twisted in her seat. "Yeah?"

"Have you ever gotten naked in a limo?"

Her smile was slow in coming, but broad and mischievous. "No."

"Want to?"

In answer, she buzzed up the panel. Alan sighed again and laid his head back. "Can't blame a guy for asking," he muttered. Especially since she'd go back to her stud stable once they returned to Savannah.

Suddenly the door opened and she bounded inside, toppling over him, laughing like a teenager. She straddled him and kissed him hard, then asked, "Do you think an hour is enough time?"

"We'll have to hit the highlights," he whispered, locking the door.

"What about the lowlights?" she said, pouting.

"In the interest of time," he murmured, pulling at her waistband, "I'll have to give them a lick and a promise."

RUNNING THROUGH the parking lot of the car-rental return, Pam yelled, "That can't *ever* happen again."

"Right," Alan yelled back. "Never."

They rushed into the building. Alan forked over an obscene deposit to a pinched-nose man in case his insurance company wouldn't cover the various damages to the limo, then they sprinted through the airport as fast as his still-aching hip would allow. When they dropped into their seats on the plane, he found it unbelievable that only a few days had passed since they'd left Savannah. It seemed like a lifetime ago—not to mention a small fortune ago, he noted wryly.

After takeoff, he donned a set of headphones, not to ignore Pam, but hoping to put some perspective on the week before they reached Savannah. Indeed, the more distant the

Fort Myers skyline became, the more painfully clear the answers seemed.

Instead of trying to dissect the roller coaster of emotions she had evoked in him this week, he simply needed to consider the facts: he had been vulnerable, she had been eager to comfort a friend. Besides, even if the circumstances were ideal—which they weren't—and even if he had the intention of taking a wife—which he didn't—he couldn't imagine any woman more unsuited to marriage than Pamela Kaminski.

Thankfully, their flight was uneventful—the little mishap when Pam sent an entire overhead bin of luggage pounding down on two passengers didn't even merit an eye twitch on his new scale of relativity. Rankling him further, she seemed oblivious to his brooding, chatting with the flight attendants and somehow managing to paint her toenails during the flight.

It was only when they were landing and he glanced over to see her death grip on the padded arms of her seat that he conceded to himself how extremely fond of her he'd become. Alan reached over to squeeze her hand, and the grateful smile she gave him made his heart lurch crazily. He knew in that moment that even if his eye healed, the tattoo was safely removed, the charges were dropped and his car insurance wasn't canceled, he still might never fully recover from his week with Pamela.

She was her usual cheery self through baggage claim and on their way back to her car, reinforcing Alan's suspicion that, for Pam, the week had simply been a casual romp— the woman had no earth-shattering revelations weighing her down. And despite the trouble that seemed to follow her around, he was going to miss her. Perhaps, he decided, after a few weeks had passed and he had shaken this somber, life-evaluating mood, he'd call her, just to see how she was doing.

He offered to call a cab, but she insisted on driving him home, saying she needed to check on some new home listings in his neighborhood, anyway. On the way, she ran two red lights, but stopped traffic on the bypass to let a mother duck and her ducklings cross.

When she pulled onto the long driveway, Alan stared at his imposing home and realized with a jolt that only one week ago, he had anticipated returning to carry his bride, Jo Montgomery, across the threshold. Now he felt almost giddy with relief at the change in circumstances. He and Jo would have been content, but not entirely happy. She had never looked at him the way she looked at John Sterling. And he owed it to himself to find a woman he could care about that much.

"Are you okay?" Pam asked, jarring him out of his reverie.

"Uh, yeah," he said, realizing she was waiting for him to get out. But when he grasped the handle, she stopped him with a hand on his arm.

"Alan," she said softly.

"Yeah," he said, his heart thudding against his chest.

"I'm sorry."

"Sorry?"

"For breaking your glasses and denting the limo and getting the ticket and having you tattooed and blacking your eye and getting you arrested."

"Twice," he amended.

"Twice," she agreed.

Her blue eyes were wide, and her upside-down mouth trembled. She was so beautiful, she was impossible to resist. He inhaled deeply and gave her a wry smile. "Forget it." Her happy grin was worth every misery he'd experienced over the week.

He opened the door and retrieved the dark suitcase she had purchased and packed for him. When he walked around to the driver's side, his mind racing for something to say, he suddenly remembered the pendant he had bought for her. "Oh, I almost forgot," he said, rooting through his gym bag until he came up with the black box. "For you."

"For me?" she asked quietly, taking her lower lip in her teeth. She slowly lifted the lid and stared at the gold sand castle, then ran her finger over the surface. "It's beautiful," she whispered, then raised shining eyes. "But why?"

Because I want you to remember me, to remember us. "Because," he said with a shrug, "I wanted to thank you for keeping me company. It was fun," he lied. It wasn't fun—it was surprising, disturbing, stimulating, stressful and amazing, but it wasn't fun.

"I love it."

She pulled the necklace from the box and fastened the clasp around her neck. The pendant disappeared into her cleavage and Alan swallowed hard.

"Thank you, Alan."

"I'll see you..." His voice trailed off because he didn't want to appear as desperately hopeful as he felt.

"Sometime," she finished for him.

"Right," he said with a nod.

"Fine," she said with a nod.

Alan watched as she rolled up the window, backed over several hundred dollars' worth of landscaping and pulled onto the road directly in the path of a luxury car whose owner stood on the brake to avoid a collision. Then, with a fluttery wave and a grind of stripped gears, she was gone.

11

PAM SLAPPED HER KNEE and laughed uproariously. "That's the best April Fool's gag I've heard today, Dr. Campbell."

Eleanor Campbell pursed her lips and steepled her fingers together over her desk. "It's no joke, Pamela. You're pregnant."

Shock, alarm and stark terror washed over her. Her throat closed and her fingers went numb. "H-how is that possible?"

Dr. Campbell smiled. "Do you want layman's terms or the scientific version?"

"Whichever will make it less true," Pam whispered. "I take my birth control pills faithfully."

"But if you had read the warning brochure for the antibiotics I prescribed for that ear infection a couple of months ago," she said sternly, "you would have known the medication can reduce the effectiveness of birth control pills." She sighed and gave Pam a sad smile. "I take it this is not a happy occasion for you and the father."

Pam closed her eyes and swallowed. "When did it happen?"

"According to the information you gave me regarding your last cycle, I'd guess on or about Valentine's Day."

If she didn't open her eyes, she decided, she wouldn't have to face it. Wouldn't have to face the fact that she was living up to the tainted Kaminski name by conceiving an illegitimate child. Wouldn't have to face the fact that life as she knew it was over. Wouldn't have to face the fact that Alan, whom she'd not seen or spoken to since returning to Savannah—and who *hated* kids—was the father of the baby growing inside her.

"MR. PARISH?" Alan's secretary's voice echoed over the speakerphone.

Alan left what had become his favorite post, the high-backed chair by the window, to push a button on his desk panel. "Yes?"

"I'm sorry, sir. Tickets to the scholarship social are sold out."

He cursed under his breath safely out of range of the microphone. "How about the hospital golf benefit?"

"Sold out."

"The lighthouse-preservation dinner?"

"Gone. The only tickets I could find for this weekend were for the podiatrists' political-action campaign dinner and the bird-watchers' society all-night skate at the roller rink."

Alan frowned. Feet or feathers—not much of a choice. "Get me two of each," he said. He dropped into his leather chair, then flipped to Pam's business card in his Rolodex—as if he hadn't memorized it. Hell, he'd dialed it twenty-eight times in the weeks since they'd returned to Savannah, but he'd always hung up before the first ring. Now he had a good excuse.

Well, maybe not good—but reasonable.

He sighed. Okay, it wasn't even reasonable, but he prayed his ploy didn't come across as desperation...even though it was.

After punching in her number, he cleared his voice, fully expecting to have to leave a message on her voice mail, but to his surprise, Pam's voice came on the line. "Hello, this is Pamela. How can I help you?"

"Uh, hi, Pam. This is Alan...Parish."

A few seconds of silence passed. "Hi, Alan. What's up?"

"Oh, not much," he said, summoning a nervous laugh. "I just called to wish you a happy April Fool's Day."

More silence, then, "That's nice."

He picked up a pen and started doodling on a pad of paper. "So, how have you been?"

"Fine, I guess," she said. "How's your eye?"

"It healed."

"And, uh, the other end?"

"Well," he said, shifting in his seat, "it's a delicate operation—I'm still trying to choose the best doctor."

"Jo told me the two of you talked things through."

"That's right." Not that there were any unresolved issues in his mind. But he knew it had made Jo feel better to explain why she had canceled their wedding.

"She seems really happy being a mom," Pam said.

He tried to concentrate on what she was saying, but he kept picturing her nude in the limo. "Yeah, can you imagine taking care of three kids?"

"Um, no, I can't."

And her breasts—God, he shuddered just thinking about them. "Just the thought sends chills up my spine."

"I remember your view on kids, Alan."

Funny, but right now he could legitimately say the most difficult part about having a baby would be sharing his wife—emotionally and physically. Pam was the kind of woman that made a man selfish. Alan shook his head to clear it. Pam, a wife? What was he thinking?

"Alan, are you still there?"

"What? Sure, I'm here." He cleared his throat. "Say,

Pam, are you free this weekend to attend a business function?''

During her few seconds of hesitation, he died a thousand times. "What kind of business function?"

His mind raced—what the devil had Linda said? "Uh, there's a feet convention at the skating rink."

"Excuse me?"

"I mean, a political fund-raiser for birds."

"What?"

Where was his brain? "Forget business—can we have dinner tonight at the River Plaza Hotel?"

"Is something wrong, Alan?"

She obviously thought the idea of them having a date was so far-fetched there had to be some other compelling reason for them to get together. "I need to talk to you...about Jo," he said, wincing at his choice of subject matter, but it was too late.

"Jo?" she asked.

"Yeah," he said, rushing ahead. "I'm having trouble working through some things and I hoped you could help me."

The silence stretched on.

"Pam?" he urged.

"Sure," she said softly. "What are friends for?"

His heart jumped for joy. "Really? I mean—" he swallowed "—that's great. Uh, seven o'clock?"

"Seven sounds fine."

She didn't sound too happy about it, but he didn't care. He just wanted to see her again. Alan's mind raced for another topic to prolong the conversation. "Have you sold the Sheridan house?"

"Not yet—Mrs. Wingate hired a poltergeist-detection team to spend the night there. We're waiting on the results. Listen, Alan, I really need to run."

"Oh, sure," he said, fighting to keep the disappointment out of his voice. "I'll see you tonight." He hung up the phone slowly, trying to be optimistic, but he'd heard the distance in her voice. Alan looked down at the pad of paper he'd been doodling on and stopped, then jammed his fingers through his hair and sighed.

He'd drawn the outline of a heart and inside, in slanting letters, he'd written the word *Pam's*.

PAM SETTLED the phone in its cradle and blinked back hot tears. How ironic that after all these weeks, he had chosen today to call. Today, when she was wrestling with how to break the news to him that he had fathered a child while on a fake honeymoon with his ex-fiancée's best friend.

How could she face him? How could she present him with the news of a child he did not want by a woman he did not want? Wouldn't the Parish family be proud. She could hear the whispers now, see the sneers on her brothers' faces.

She dropped her head into her hands. How could she face Jo? Since Pam's return, her friend had thanked her profusely for offering Alan a comforting hand during a very trying period in his life. Only it would soon become clear that she had offered Alan more than her hand.

How could she face her child? How could she tell her child that he or she was conceived in lust by a father who had just been jilted and by a mother whose dreams were too outlandish to be realized?

And how could she face herself? She had been careless with her heart, and careless with her body. She had known Alan was in love with her best friend. He'd used her to get over the hurt, and she had let him. She had let him on the slimmest hope that the man who represented everything she wanted in a partner—security, integrity, heritage and nobility—would recognize in her what no man had ever seen and fall in love with her.

Perhaps she had loved him ever since he'd hauled her off Mary Jane Cunningham's back in high school. He had taken up for her, but she'd given him a shin-shiner because she didn't know how else to react to someone in his social class. She couldn't very well act as though she *liked* him.

Since that day, she had found it easier to make fun of him rather than admit he had something she envied. And when their paths had crossed again as adults, she had simply picked up where she'd left off. Only in the wee hours of the morning when she was alone with her thoughts and fears and dreams had she been honest with herself. Only then had she admitted that Alan was the man she wanted but knew she'd never have, so she'd filled her dance card with has-beens and wannabes and never-would-bes.

Just like Alan had filled his dance card with her in the wake of Jo's rejection.

She shoved her hands into her hair. Now what? Pam wiped her eyes and pulled her address book from a desk drawer. After dialing an Atlanta extension, she sniffed mightily, feeling better just at the anticipation of hearing the voice of a dear old friend. Someone with a little objective distance. Someone she could trust to set her straight. Someone with big, broad, undemanding shoulders.

"Hello?"

"Manny? It's Pamela."

"Well, hello, baby doll!" He clucked. "You'd better have a good excuse why I haven't heard from you lately."

She smiled at the laughter in his voice. "Would you settle for a good excuse for calling now?" As much as she tried to maintain control, she could not keep her voice from breaking on the last word.

"What's wrong?" he asked, immediately serious. "Oh,

God, it's a man, isn't it?'' He sighed dramatically. "The straight ones all seem programmed to seek and destroy.''

"I need to get away for a few days,'' she whispered.

"I'll alert the pedestrians of Atlanta that you're on your way.''

ALAN CHECKED his watch for the twentieth time. Where was she? Pam was only a few minutes late, but after he'd talked to her, the rest of the afternoon had crawled. He was impatient to see her, to talk to her. He drummed on the surface of the hotel bar, feeling ready to come out of his skin with anticipation. The bartender slid a shot of whiskey across the bar and he downed it, hoping it would give him the courage he needed.

He loved her. It sounded ridiculous and she'd probably laugh in his face, but he didn't care. The week in Fort Myers, although admittedly fraught with disaster, had given him a taste of her spice for life, and he had become addicted. Every day since returning home, he had told himself the restlessness would pass, that they had simply been caught up in the romance of a beach fling. But he finally had to admit to himself that he wanted Pamela, that he *needed* Pamela in his life.

And he refused to share her with other men—he wanted a commitment. Marriage seemed a bit ludicrous considering he had been standing at the altar with another woman just a few weeks ago. Besides, Pam had made it perfectly clear that she wasn't looking to become anyone's wife. But he hoped she would at least move in with him, a public declaration that they were a couple. Then perhaps someday they would both be ready for marriage…and a family.

Alan stopped and shook his head. He still had to get through tonight—he'd worry about the heavy stuff later. His imminent concern was the risk of her choking from laughing too hard. In his mind he reviewed the Heimlich maneuver, then checked his watch again. She was worth waiting for.

AROUND EIGHT O'CLOCK Pam found a parking place a half block from Manny's apartment building. Her back ached and her feet were swollen from the five-hour drive, an omen of the months to come, she knew. She'd cried off her makeup by the time she'd reached Macon, but Manny wouldn't mind. City sounds greeted her when she opened the door and lifted herself out of the car. Little Five Points was one of her favorite areas in Atlanta, and ablaze with crimson, pink and white azaleas, it was certainly one of the prettiest this time of year.

She rolled her shoulders and stretched her legs, then grabbed her bag. Although it was only a short walk to Manny's building, followed by a brief flight of stairs, her feet felt as though they were made of concrete by the time she arrived at her friend's apartment. He swung open the door before she'd finished knocking and swept her into a huge hug.

When he set her on her feet, he chucked her lightly under the chin. "Pam, one of these days you simply must begin to age."

Pam smiled at the tall, fair-haired man she'd met at a club several years ago. They'd hit it off and had maintained contact over the years, visiting at every chance. Manny Oliver was a confirmed homosexual and a world-class good guy. Pam looked at his dancing eyes and sighed. "Manny, if you ever decide to jump ship, I want to be the first to know."

"Darling, you and Ellie would be the only women in my lifeboat."

"How is Ellie?" Pam asked, referring to his former roommate.

"Disgustingly happy," he said, rolling his eyes. "Married less than a year and she and Mark are already expecting a baby." He shuddered. "I ask you—what woman could possibly endure those hideous maternity fashions?"

Pam pursed her lips and dropped her gaze. "Got any dos and don'ts for me?"

"Oh, no," he murmured, sinking into a chair. "Not you, too."

She nodded, her eyes welling with tears.

He simply opened his arms and shooed her inside, then rocked her through another crying jag. Only after she'd blown her nose twice and gotten over the hiccups did he question her.

"Who is the proud papa?"

"His name is Alan Parish."

"Does he know?"

She shook her head.

"Are you going to tell him?"

Pam nodded.

"*Tell* me this guy is husband material."

She laughed dryly. "He had a wedding in February."

"Pam," he chided. "Even *I* don't mess around with married men."

"No, he was marrying my best friend, but she called off the wedding at the last minute."

"Ah. And you picked up the pieces?"

"Something like that. But I don't think he's ready to make another trip to the altar." She laughed softly, then added, "Not with me anyway."

"How do you think he will react to the news?"

She bit her bottom lip to stem another flood of tears. "He hates kids."

Manny frowned. "Well, if that's the case, he should keep his pants zipped."

"It's my fault—my pills failed."

"That's a moot point. Now you have to make plans for this baby. Are you going to keep it or give it up for adoption?"

"I'm keeping it."

"And can you expect any help from this Parish guy?"

"I'm not sure."

Manny squinted and angled his head. "Pam, is there something you're not telling me?"

"I'm in love with him."

"The plot thickens. And his feelings for you?"

"Zilch."

"Not true—he got naked with you, didn't he?"

"Okay, I suppose he's physically attracted to me."

"It's a start."

"But he's still in love with my best friend."

"He told you this?"

"No, but he hasn't called since we were together—until today when he asked me to meet so we could talk about his feelings for her."

"Sounds like a jerk to me."

"Oh, no—he's really a great guy. In fact, one of the reasons I admire him so much is that he was so committed to my friend."

"If the man doesn't scoop you up and count his blessings, he's obtuse," Manny insisted.

"He's a little uptight," Pam admitted, smiling fondly. "But when he lets go, he can be very endearing."

Manny handed her a cup of tea and lifted one eyebrow. "And good in bed, I certainly hope."

She nodded miserably.

He sighed. "Promise me you won't wear stripes in the last trimester."

ALAN STRUGGLED to keep his voice calm. "But you don't understand," he explained to the receptionist at Pam's office. "I *have* left voice-mail messages. I've left *fourteen* voice-mail messages."

"Perhaps her cellular phone—"

"She's not answering. Pam was supposed to meet me last night and she didn't show. I'm worried about her."

The receptionist didn't seem particularly sympathetic that he'd been stood up. "Sir, all I can tell you is that Ms. Kaminski said she'd be out of the office for a few days. I can give you her pager number—"

"I called her pager number—she's not answering!"

"Then I'll transfer you to her voice mail."

"Wait—" he yelled, but he heard a click and Pam's voice message, which he'd now memorized. Alan slammed down the phone and cursed. He reared back and kicked his desk as hard as he could, bellowing when the pain shot up his leg.

"Mr. Parish," Linda said, sticking her head through his doorway. "Are you okay?"

Alan inhaled deeply. "I'm fine, Linda." Then he limped to his valet and yanked on his jacket. "Cancel my appointments for the rest of the afternoon."

PAMELA LIVED IN a neat little town house in an artsy part of town—Alan suspected she'd made a good investment, considering her line of work. He had been there only twice to pick her up for some event they had attended together, but he hadn't gone inside. The tiny driveway was vacant, and the shades were drawn. The outside light glowed weakly in the bright midmorning sun, as if to fool someone into thinking she was home.

He walked up the steps and retrieved her untouched morning paper, then knocked on her front door several times before going around to the back and doing the same. After ten minutes, Alan climbed back into his car and pounded his steering wheel in frustration. "Pam, where are you?" he shouted into the cab of his car. *"Where are you?"*

He laid his head back and exhaled, then straightened and turned the key. Within minutes, he was heading toward Jo Montgomery's office, not sure what he was going to tell her, but absolutely certain that he had to find Pam.

As luck would have it, Jo was in a deep embrace with her new husband, John Sterling, when Alan knocked and stuck his head through her open doorway. They quickly parted, although John kept a possessive arm around Jo's waist while she straightened her clothing.

"Alan," she gasped. "What a nice surprise."

"We didn't hear you come in," John said with a tight smile.

"I wonder why," Alan said dryly. "Jo, could I have a word with you?"

"Of course," she said quickly, then glanced at her husband, who wore a wary frown.

"It's about Pam," Alan informed him impatiently.

"Jo, I'll see you at home," John said, dropping a quick kiss on her mouth. He nodded curtly to Alan as he left.

"Do you want some coffee?" Jo asked politely.

Alan shook his head. "I'm looking for Pam and I thought you might know where she is."

Jo averted her gaze and relief swept through him. Jo knew, which meant at least Pam was okay.

"Did you leave her a voice message?" she asked.

"Sure did."

"Maybe she hasn't had a chance to return calls."

"Where is she?"

"Alan—"

"I have to see her, Jo. It's important."

"She asked me not to tell anyone—"

"Jo, there's something you should know."

Jo frowned. "Alan, what's wrong?"

He exhaled noisily, suddenly unsure of himself. "Something happened when Pam and I were in Fort Myers."

"Alan, I don't think this is any of my—"

"I fell in love with her."

Her eyes widened slightly, and a slow smile climbed her face. "What?"

"I fell in love with her." He raised his hands in the air. "Jo, I swear to you on everything I hold sacred that nothing ever went on between us when you and I were together." He pursed his lips and gritted his teeth before continuing. "But when we were in Fort Myers, I saw Pam in a new light. She's warm and funny and smart—" He broke off and shrugged helplessly. "She makes me happy, Jo, and when I'm with her, I understand what you must feel when you're with John."

Jo's eyes were full of unshed tears. "Alan, nothing would make me happier than to see the two of you together."

"I have to find her, Jo, and tell her how I feel. Even if she doesn't love me, I can't go another day with this on my heart."

She smiled, displaying a dimple. "How about five hours?"

"Five hours?"

"She's in Atlanta, staying with a friend for a few days."

Alan frowned. "A male friend?"

She nodded, and hurt stabbed him hard in the chest. He laughed softly and shook his head. "What's the point if she's with another man?"

Jo walked over to him and touched his arm. "It's a good thing John didn't let that stop him," she said quietly. "For both our sakes."

12

AFTER A MORNING of hugging the toilet, Pam napped away the afternoon, then dragged herself toward the tub. A shower, she'd discovered, was a heartbroken, pregnant woman's solace because there she could cry freely and it didn't matter.

Not that she didn't cry everywhere else anyway. Throughout the day, Manny pampered her with cool cloths for her forehead, warm cloths for her neck, pillows for her feet, pillows for her back, the latest magazines and nice, bland food when her stomach could stand it. She felt lumpy and frumpy in one of Manny's old sweat suits, but being enveloped in his big, masculine clothes gave her comfort.

When dusk began to fall, he dragged a cushiony chair out onto the fire escape and planted her there while he brushed her hair. The spring breeze was unusually balmy, inspiring Pam to inhale great lungfuls of fresh air. A zillion stars glittered overhead, triggering memories of the night she and Alan strolled along the moonlit beach and the passion that had swept them away.

Well, actually, Alan had been swept away to jail, but that night had been an awakening for her, and she would never forget it. She toyed with the sand-castle pendant that hung around her neck, where it had been since the day they'd returned to Savannah.

"Maybe I need a change of scenery," she said, sipping the cup of peppermint tea Manny had prepared for her.

"You're welcome to this apartment," he offered. "But in a couple of months you'll have to find another roommate."

She twisted in her chair. "You're moving?"

"To San Francisco, in June."

"Why didn't you say something?" Pam demanded.

"Darlin', you've got enough on your mind." He clucked. "I was planning to send you a change-of-address card."

"What's in San Francisco?"

"A career path," he said flatly. "On New Year's I took a glimpse into my future, and believe me, there's nothing pretty about a senior-citizen drag-queen performer."

Pam laughed—Manny hadn't yet seen his fortieth birthday and was an exceptionally handsome guy. "What will you do?"

He bowed. "Concierge at the Chandelier House, at your service, madam."

"Manny, that's wonderful—you'll be a big hit!" Then she made a face. "I'll miss you though."

"You and the *bébé* will have to come out for a visit."

"We will," she declared, grinning at him in the mirror.

Manny cocked his ear toward the apartment and held up a finger. "I think I heard a knock, I'll be right back."

Pam sank deeper into the seat and wrapped her hands over her stomach. *Imagine,* she thought with a little smile, *Alan's baby growing inside me.* And although she wasn't foolish enough to believe raising a child on her own would be easy, she would do what she had done all her life— make the best of her circumstances. This child would be loved, if by no one else, then by her.

"Pam," Manny said from the doorway, "you have a visitor."

She jerked her head around in surprise, then gasped when

she saw Alan standing in the living room, his suit jacket over his shoulder and his face grim. To see him after so many weeks was a shock to her senses, and she couldn't fathom why he was here. Standing on wobbly legs, she stepped into the doorway, aware that Manny hovered an arm's length behind her.

Alan straightened when Pam stepped into view. His heart slammed against his chest painfully. She looked beautiful, but different. Softer, perhaps, with no makeup and her hair loose around her shoulders. Wearing her lover's clothes, she looked dewy-eyed and vulnerable. Jealousy ripped through him and he tried not to think about the rumpled covers and pillows on the couch. Seeing their recent sex venue only strengthened his resolve that under no circumstances would he share her with another man.

"Alan, this is my friend Manny—"

"We already met, sweetheart," Manny assured her, but his eyes never left Alan.

Alan's hands twitched at the casual term of endearment, but he tried to focus on the reason he'd come.

"Alan," Pam asked, taking another step toward him. "What are you doing here?"

"Looking for you."

Her smile was shaky. "Obviously, but why?"

Alan glanced to her tall boyfriend, but the man wasn't about to budge from the room. "Would you excuse us, um, Manny?"

The guy poked his tongue into his cheek, then glanced to Pam with raised eyebrows for confirmation. She nodded.

"I'll be in the bedroom," the man said, glaring at Alan. "Yell if you need me, Pam."

"Thanks, Manny."

Alan waited until he heard the bedroom door close before

speaking, and then he didn't know where to start. "I waited for you the other night."

"Something came up—I should have called."

"I was worried."

"I'm fine," she said with a nervous laugh. "How did you know where to find me?"

"Jo."

She nodded, lowering her gaze.

"Look, Pam," he said, stepping closer but maintaining a safe distance. "I didn't mean to embarrass you in front of your boyfriend, but—"

"He's not my boyfriend. Manny's gay."

Relief swept through him. "Really? Hey, that's great— I say a man's got to do what a man's got to do, and if that means marching—"

"Alan, what do you want?"

He mentally went down the list he'd made and left in the car. "I didn't mean to embarrass you in front of your boyfriend—"

"You said that already," she said, lifting a corner of her mouth. "Don't tell me you've got a script."

Panic flooded his vocal cords. "I love you, dammit!"

She stood stock-still while he hung out swinging in the breeze, waiting for her answer. Seconds ticked by.

"Say something," he said.

"I'm pregnant with your baby."

He froze and glanced around the room, absorbing her words, but finding them too unbelievable to comprehend. "Come again?"

"I'm pregnant with your baby."

Strange, but the words sounded exactly the same the second time. Alan felt his jaw drop, close, then drop again. Intelligent words to combine into an appropriate response had to reside somewhere deep in his brain, but they didn't seem to be forthcoming.

She waited.

His mind raced. Men became fathers every day—coming up with a reply for the woman he loved couldn't be that hard.

"Gee," he said with a shaky laugh, then felt the room close in around him. "I think I'm going to pass out." But even though the trip to the floor seemed to be in slow motion, the thump of his head against the wood revived him somewhat.

Alan heard Pam scream for Manny, then heard the man tell her to get a pitcher of water from the refrigerator.

Manny slapped him lightly on the cheeks, then a stinging blast of ice water hit his face, taking his breath. His temple throbbed with a new pain.

His eyes popped open and through his water-speckled lenses, he saw Pam standing over him holding a glass pitcher.

"Uh—Pam," Manny said. "You could have taken out the ice first." He handed her a chunk as large as a man's fist, tinged with blood. "He might have a concussion."

"I'm fine," Alan mumbled. "Help me up."

Manny helped him to the couch then gave him a cloth to hold to his bleeding temple. "You're going to have a heck of a goose egg, man."

Alan smiled and shrugged, looking at Pam. "It comes with the territory."

"I hope your insurance is paid up," Manny muttered on his way out of the room.

"Sounds like I'm going to need the family plan," Alan said, locking gazes with Pam.

"Alan—"

"Why didn't you tell me about the baby?" He clasped

her by the upper arms. "I've missed you like crazy these past few weeks, and I was nearly insane wondering what happened to you last night."

"When you called, I was trying to decide how to break the news, then you said you wanted to talk about your feelings for Jo—"

"It was an excuse—I didn't think you'd meet me otherwise."

She blinked. "That was dumb."

"I was desperate!"

Pam winced. "How much does Jo know?"

"Everything."

"Oh no."

"And she said she couldn't be happier. In fact, she encouraged me to come after you." His Adam's apple bobbed. "Pamela Kaminski, will you marry me?"

Her eyes widened. "M-marry?"

"You know—you'd be the wife, I'd be the husband."

"Wife?" she whispered, then smiled tremulously. "I hadn't planned on ever being anyone's wife." Then she laughed, her eyes filling with tears. "But I hadn't planned on ever being anyone's mother, either."

He grinned. "I've noticed lately that life is full of surprises."

"Alan, I know you don't like kids—"

"Unless they're mine," he corrected.

"But kids are loud..."

"So are you."

"—and messy..."

"So are you."

"—and the diapers..."

He winced. "You got me there."

"It won't be easy."

Alan curled his fingers around her neck and pulled her face close to his. "Is that a yes?"

Her eyes were luminous as she studied his face, then she dabbed at the blood on his temple. "That's a yes," she whispered, then added, "The 'P' stands for 'papa.'"

THE CHURCH WAS somewhat less crowded this time, Alan noticed from his view at the altar. Which was fine with him, as long as the people who mattered were there.

His parents sat on the front pew, crying happy tears because Pam had enchanted them as much as she had enchanted him. Pam's mother sat on the opposite side, dabbing her eyes. Her two brothers stood next to him, fingering their tight collars, waiting for Pam to make her entrance. Her older brother, Roy, pointed to Alan's bandaged hand. "What happened?"

"A little mishap when we tried on rings," Alan explained with a shrug.

"Sounds like Pam," Roy affirmed with a nod. "You'd better lower your deductible. By the way, where the devil is she?"

Alan tried not to betray the nervousness that wallowed in his stomach. "She must be here, or the director wouldn't have let them start the music."

"They've played that song so many times, I know it by heart," Roy whispered hoarsely.

"Maybe she had a sudden case of morning sickness," Alan said, trying to squelch humiliating flashbacks from the last time he stood at the altar.

"It's two in the afternoon."

"Well, you know women's bodies can be...unpredictable."

Roy grinned. "Not the word I would have used, but whatever."

After another five minutes of "O Promise Me", Alan glanced at Jo, who stood an arm's length away in a simple bridesmaid dress. She chewed on her lower lip and shrugged slightly, then mouthed, "Want me to go check?"

Alan sighed, feeling sick to his stomach. If Pam had changed her mind about becoming his wife, he wanted to be the one to know. He walked down the aisle, trying to block out the concerned murmur that swept through the guests, then marched through the back doors of the chapel.

His hand shook as he opened the door to the bride's waiting room, and his heart pounded when he saw it was empty. He checked the bathroom, but found it abandoned, as well. With a sinking heart, he realized she must have changed her mind. He gritted his teeth, then laughed bitterly. He was zero for two.

His eyes stung with emotion as he walked back toward the chapel once again to tell everyone to go home, but as he walked past the open doors of the church entrance, he heard a familiar beeping horn. He glanced outside in time to see Pam's Volvo jump the curb and come to a screeching halt, mere inches from a stone statue of some important-looking saint.

Dressed in full bridal regalia, with a voluminous veil and enormous train, she took quite a while to extricate herself from the car. When she did, she gathered the skirt in her arms, hiking it up to her thighs to run across the churchyard in bare feet. Carrying her shoes in one hand, she waved when she saw him in the doorway. "I'm coming!" she yelled. "I'm coming!"

"Where have you been?" he demanded when she came to a halt in front of him. God, she was gorgeous, especially with her slightly rounded tummy.

"Mrs. Wingate paged me," she said breathlessly. "Her head psychic told her she had a one-hour window of safety to buy the Sheridan house." She panted for air. "I was already dressed, and I figured I could leave and get the papers signed before anyone missed me." She smiled happily, her chest heaving. "Did anyone miss me?"

He sighed, wanting to shake her. "You scared me to death—I thought you had changed your mind."

She looped her arms around his neck. "Not on your life—you're stuck with me, Mr. Alan P. Parish." She pulled his mouth to hers for a deep kiss.

He raised his head, then bent down and lifted her into his arms. "Let's go make you my wife before anything else happens." Then he turned, carried her toward the chapel and whispered, "I have a confession to make."

"What?"

"I told the guy at the tattoo parlor that the 'P' stands for 'Pam's.'"

Epilogue

ALAN RAISED his hands. "Pam," he said in a soothing voice. "Put down the nail file."

"*You!*" she yelled at him from the hospital bed. "You did this to me!"

"Honey," he said, "don't you think it was a combined effort?"

He ducked as the vase of flowers flew past his head and crashed against the wall at his back.

"You're right!" he affirmed hurriedly, raising his arms in surrender. He put on a mournful expression and gestured vaguely toward her huge stomach. "It's all my fault—I did this to you and I am the lowest scum on the face of the earth."

Her face contorted with pain and Alan's heart twisted in agony. His beautiful wife was lying in abject misery, and he couldn't even get close enough to the hospital bed to practice the Lamaze they had learned together.

"Do you have your focus point, sweetie?" he called, inching closer.

She lay back, panting, then pinned him with a deadly look. "I'm focusing on a life of celibacy!"

"Honey, you don't mean that," he said in his most cajoling voice, but stopped when she held up the makeshift dagger. "Celibacy is good," he assured her with a nervous laugh. "We can make it work." Alan retreated the few inches he'd advanced. "How about an ice chip?" he asked.

"How about I chip your tooth?" she offered, smiling sweetly.

The door swung open and Dr. Campbell strode in with a smile. "How're we doing?"

Alan, weak with relief to have an ally, smiled broadly. "Just great," he said, then glanced at Pam's murderous expression. "I mean, not very well at all."

"Let's see where you are, Pam." To Alan's alarm, the doctor eased Pam's swollen feet and ankles into the stirrups, giving him a bird's-eye view beneath her hospital gown.   He swallowed and cleared his throat. "I think I'll wait outside."

"Oh no you don't," Pam said, ominously. "You're not going anywhere."

Alan nodded obediently and wiped his sweaty hands on his slacks. "Right—wild horses couldn't drag me out of here."

The doctor glanced at the monitor. "Here comes another contraction, Pam. Just try to relax."

"Remember to breathe, sweetie," Alan called. "Hee-hee—"

"Shut up!" she shouted.

"I'm shutting up," he said, nodding vigorously.

"If the pain's getting to be too much," the doctor said to Pam, "I can go ahead and give you an epidural."

"Thanks anyway, Dr. Campbell," Alan said from the wall. "We decided from the beginning to go for natural childbir—"

"Give me the needle, Dr. C.," Pam cut in, "and I'll give it to myself."

"Oh my," the doctor said, moving her hands beneath the gown.

Alan glanced over, then squeezed his eyes shut, muttering thanks to the heavens for the thousandth time today that he was not a woman.

"Forget the epidural," the doctor said, depressing the nurse call button with her elbow. "You're ready to start pushing."

Alan's eyes popped open. "Already?"

"Already?" Pam shrieked. "It's been nine hours!"

But I'm not ready, I'm not wise enough yet to be a father. Perspiration popped out on his hairline and panic rose in his chest, suffocating him.

The nurses rushed in and dressed him in sanitary garb as if he were a kid going out in the snow. He was relegated, happily, to a corner as they prepared Pam for the final stages of labor. Alan had never felt so guilty and helpless in his life. She agonized through two more contractions before the doctor said, "Daddy, you come jump in anytime."

Alan glanced to Pam for affirmation, but her eyes were squeezed shut to ward off the pain. Her hands were on the bed railing, so at least her weapon had been confiscated.

"Pam?" he said weakly, stepping closer. "Sweetie?"

She didn't open her eyes, but she lifted a hand toward him, and he went to her side with relief.

"Alan," she whispered, lolling her head toward him.

"Yes, dear?"

"What does the 'P' stand for?"

"Pam, now doesn't seem like the time—"

She twisted a handful of his shirt and pulled him close to her. "I said, what does the 'P' stand for?"

"Pam, you need to push," Dr. Campbell said. "On the count of three."

"Alan—" Pam said through clenched teeth.

"One—"

"—what does—" Her face reddened.

"—two—"

"—*the 'P' stand for?*"

"—three—push!"

Her face contorted in pain and she screamed. Alan, scared half out of his wits, yelled, "Presley! The 'P' stands for 'Presley!'"

She grunted, bearing down for several seconds, then relaxed on the pillow and opened her eyes. "Presley?" she panted.

He nodded miserably. "My mom was a huge fan."

She laughed between gasping for air, readying herself for another push at the doctor's urging. He held her hand tight and whispered loving words in her ear.

"Here comes the head," said the doctor.

She bore down and squeezed his hand until he was sure she'd broken several bones. His heart thrashed in his chest and he looked around to see what he would hit when he passed out.

"One more push, Pam," the doctor urged.

She took a deep breath and screamed loud enough to rattle the windows. Alan held on, wondering if his hearing would return.

"Here we are," the doctor said triumphantly. "It's a big boy."

Relief and elation flooded his chest and he kissed Pam's face, whispering, "It's a boy. It's a boy."

Pam, exhausted but beaming, held her hands out to accept the wrinkled, outraged infant. Alan's heart filled to bursting as he looked down at his son, whose lusty cries filled the air.

"Do you have a name?" the doctor asked.

"Not yet—" he said.

"Of course we do," Pam said as she raised her moist gaze to her husband. "His name is Presley."

Take 4 bestselling love stories FREE

Plus get a FREE surprise gift!

Special Limited-time Offer

Mail to Harlequin Reader Service®

3010 Walden Avenue
P.O. Box 1867
Buffalo, N.Y. 14240-1867

YES! Please send me 4 free Harlequin Love and Laughter™ novels and my free surprise gift. Then send me 4 brand-new novels every other month, which I will receive months before they appear in bookstores. Bill me at the low price of $2.90 each plus 25¢ delivery per book and applicable sales tax if any*. That's the complete price and a savings of over 10% off the cover prices—quite a bargain! I understand that accepting the books and gift places me under no obligation ever to buy any books. I can always return a shipment and cancel at any time. Even if I never buy another book from Harlequin, the 4 free books and the surprise gift are mine to keep forever.

102 BPA A7EF

Name	(PLEASE PRINT)	
Address	Apt. No.	
City	State	Zip

This offer is limited to one order per household and not valid to present Love and Laughter™ subscribers. *Terms and prices are subject to change without notice. Sales tax applicable in N.Y.

ULL-397

©1996 Harlequin Enterprises Limited

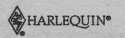

As Seen on TV!

Free Gift Offer

With a Free Gift proof-of-purchase
from any Harlequin® book, you can receive
a beautiful cubic zirconia pendant.

This stunning marquise-shaped stone is a genuine cubic
zirconia—accented by an 18" gold tone necklace.
(Approximate retail value $19.95)

Send for yours today...
compliments of ◆HARLEQUIN®

To receive your free gift, a cubic zirconia pendant, send us one original proof-of-purchase, photocopies not accepted, from the back of any Harlequin Romance®, Harlequin Presents®, Harlequin Temptation®, Harlequin Superromance®, Harlequin Love & Laughter®, Harlequin Intrigue®, Harlequin American Romance®, or Harlequin Historicals® title available at your favorite retail outlet, together with the Free Gift Certificate, plus a check or money order for $1.65 U.S./$2.15 CAN. (do not send cash) to cover postage and handling, payable to Harlequin Free Gift Offer. We will send you the specified gift. Allow 6 to 8 weeks for delivery. Offer good until March 31, 1998, or while quantities last. Offer valid in the U.S. and Canada only.

Free Gift Certificate

Name: _____

Address: _____

City: _____ State/Province: _____ Zip/Postal Code: _____

Mail this certificate, one proof-of-purchase and a check or money order for postage and handling to: HARLEQUIN FREE GIFT OFFER 1998. In the U.S.: 3010 Walden Avenue, P.O. Box 9071, Buffalo NY 14269-9057. In Canada: P.O. Box 604, Fort Erie, Ontario L2Z 5X3.

FREE GIFT OFFER   084-KEZ

ONE PROOF-OF-PURCHASE
To collect your fabulous FREE GIFT, a cubic zirconia pendant, you must include this
original proof-of-purchase for each gift with the properly completed Free Gift Certificate.

084-KEZR2